THE GOLDEN
CREEP

By George Bagby

THE GOLDEN CREEP

George Bagby

M

5/82

PUBLISHED FOR THE CRIME CLUB BY

DOUBLEDAY & COMPANY, INC.

GARDEN CITY, NEW YORK

1982

All of the characters in this book
are fictitious, and any resemblance
to actual persons, living or dead,
is purely coincidental.

Library of Congress Cataloging in Publication Data

Bagby, George, 1906–
The golden creep.

I. Title.
PS3537.T3184G6   813'.52
AACR2
ISBN 0-385-18142-6
Library of Congress Catalog Card Number 81–43913

First Edition

For

Wilma and Joe Pfeiler

THE GOLDEN
CREEP

CHAPTER 1

I don't expect that my good, old friend, Inspector Schmidt, will ever understand. To him it was nothing more than just another sleazy dump, a place for dim-witted yokels. He told me as much. He was prepared to concede that George Bagby, New York-born and -bred, was no yokel; but he was quick to add that he was giving no guarantees that I had not become dim-witted.

The fact that in the inspector's company I had been in places much like it, more of them than I can count, was no defense. The inspector is the New York Police Department's Chief of Homicide. Trailing after him to observe his investigations against the day when I would be writing about them, I inevitably find myself in places which, but for the necessities of investigation, no reasonably sophisticated man would frequent.

In the hope that he might understand, I have tried again and again to turn him on to Christopher Marlowe, but I made the mistake of telling him that it was widely accepted that Kit Marlowe had come to an untimely end, stabbed in a tavern brawl. He fastened on that and he has ever since argued that this circumstance alone should have told me that The Topless Towers was no place for George Bagby.

"You might have known," he says, "that a place

that's anyway connected with a barroom brawler has to be a place where you could do yourself no good."

What it comes down to, I suppose, is that I was hooked on the mighty line. It was a nightclub. Beyond any question it did look like a sleazy dump. It was, however, called The Topless Towers and it featured a stand-up comic called The Face. No name—just The Face or, more fully, The Face That Launched a Thousand Quips.

I quoted to Schmitty those great words Marlowe wrote for Faustus in the scene where Mephistopheles gave the fallen philosopher a look at Helen of Troy:

"Was this the face that launch'd a thousand ships,
   And burnt the topless towers of Ilium?"

The inspector, of course, didn't actually think I had waltzed into the joint in the hope that I might run into Grecian Helen, but he took inordinate pleasure in accusing me of just such imbecility. It was no more than curiosity that had taken me in there. A dump that looked so honky-tonk while it was tossing out references to the Marlowe masterpiece—the incongruity of it was haunting. Inevitably I got sucked in.

The Topless Towers were show girls, and they were as advertised both in adjective and noun. They were topless. That they were only gauzily removed from being bottomless as well was something of an unadvertised bonus. I haven't done any special study of Marlowe in quest of words that might have served for that. There may be some, but I don't know of them.

As squads of show girls go, they were extraordinary. Monumentality is not unknown in that field of endeavor, but these were babes who could without exaggeration be called towers. They were built and, as The Face was given to saying, they were built for basketball. Six foot and better all of them, in heels they were way up where they could eat apples off the bald heads of all but the tallest patrons.

Apart from The Face, the show was a heaping portion of nothing much. The Towers strutted and they undulated. The evident fact that they afflicted the customers with carnal desires I found interesting only because it mystified me. How carnal can a man be when positioned on a stepladder?

The Face was funny. He was short and tubby. On stage, of course, he was dwarfed by the Towers but, even when he came offstage, he was short and tubby. He had all the gags that had been polished on burlesque stages over so long a time that they had been worn threadbare; but again and again, just short of the point where I had a yawn coming on, he would slip in a new-minted impertinence. Those invariably bounced off the walls. It was obvious that he put them in just for himself.

I quickly got to know him. He was on when I came in. So that time around I caught only part of his routine. As soon as he'd wound it up and came off for a break, he headed straight for me.

"You laugh selectively," he said. "For that I've got to buy you a drink."

"One of these drinks?" I said. "Thanks, but you'll be wasting your money."

"Weak?"

"In time of water shortage—criminal."

"Jocko is not without talent. His mickeys are much admired. Those come full strength."

"For laughing selectively?" I asked. "That rates me a mickey?"

"For washing your face," he said. "What you have in

your glass does wonders for the complexion. So tell me what it is you're not drinking."

"Bourbon and water," I said. "No ice."

"For Bourbon and branch you should talk hush puppy," he said. "For no fizz and no rocks you should talk Oxbridge. You don't talk either. So what are you?"

"Just a guy who likes the taste of whiskey. Bubbles and ice get between taste buds and taste."

He crooked a finger and the bartender came hurrying over. Lifting the glass out of my hand, the little man shoved it at the barkeep.

"Take this away," he said. "We have here a gentleman who knows what whiskey tastes like. Make him a drink. On this one think brown water and white Bourbon and you'll come out just about right. Bring me my usual."

The bartender scuttled off. It was virtually no time before he sent a waiter over with the drinks. What he'd made for me was more than a simple reversal of his customary proportions. He had outdone himself. I had something that came so close to straight whiskey as made no difference. The drink I'd bought had not been totally innocent of booze. It had been close but not total. This one seemed to be innocent of water.

"That guy's an overachiever," I said.

"He eats out of my hand."

That was obvious. At a word from The Face the barman had all but kowtowed.

I switched to what was on my mind. "Tell me about this club of yours," I said. "How did Marlowe get into the act?"

"What would you want for a saloon? Alfred Lord Tennyson? A. A. Milne?"

"The Pooh Bar would never have brought me in off the street," I said.

"So you prefer Christopher Marlowe to Christopher Robin and that figures," The Face said. "Since you don't look like a professor of English lit., what does it leave? You've got to be a poet."

"Not even close," I said. "I'm a crime writer."

"So maybe that figures too. This club is a crime."

"Does the management like you running it down?"

"I don't just run it down. I also run it. I'm the management."

"Absentee owner?" I asked.

"Who's absent? I'm here."

"You own it. You work in it. You don't like it," I said. "Why don't you do something about changing it?"

"Just the way it is it brings in a pretty buck and I like the pretty buck. I change it to the way you'll like it and I'll like it and then what'll it be? I'll be closing the doors. You and me, we're not the big spenders. We want whiskey in our water and wit in our entertainment. You can't run a club for the likes of us. You run a club for these types that come begging to be taken."

"I don't know," I said. "There are places."

"Big overhead and low take," he said.

His attention drifted off to a patron who was just coming in the door. This was a patron who warranted attention. The sight of him should have brought a gleam of greed into any nightclub owner's eye. The Face showed no such gleam. I could read his expression as nothing but disdain. Evidences of greed, however, were not absent. The bartender took off from his tending to throw the guy the big smile and the welcoming wave. The piano player abandoned the tune he was playing, breaking away from it in midmeasure to launch into "Tea for Two." The newcomer acknowledged. It was a handwave for the bartender and a hipwave for the pianist. Meanwhile the hatcheck girl was all aflutter as she took the man's coat. That was a lot of coat—black mink with a lining that could have come off a pool table if pool tables were covered in satin.

With his left hand he was patting the girl's behind while in his right he flourished a bill. From where I sat it looked like a twenty. I could see that it looked good to the girl. She reached for it, but the guy had his own way of tipping. Eluding her clutching hand, he stuffed the bill down her bosom.

"The Golden Creep," The Face muttered, "and no place to hide."

"What about the pretty buck?" I asked.

"It comes better," he said, "from customers who know their place."

The man headed straight for us. At a table he passed on his way he picked up an empty chair and brought it along with him. He set it down and settled himself on it. He sat so that he was all but on top of The Face while he was offering me not much more than his back.

The guy looked to be somewhere in his fifties and fighting it. His was the look of ruddy poor health. He was broader in the hip than in the shoulder, and his color was that yellowish pink that suggests an overripe peach. He also had a soft look. With his face turned away from me, he was offering for my inspection the hair at the back of his head. He had a lot of it and none of it was the color of hair. It was a dye job but a fancy one—a pale red artfully streaked with yellow.

The Face offered no greeting.

"Who asked you to sit down?" he said.

"Now, look," the man said. "Be serious."

"I'm offstage," The Face said, "so I'm serious. I don't make with the funnies unless I'm on."

"You spoke to her?"

"Probably not. I never talk to them any more than I have to. They have no conversation."

"You know what I mean."

"I know that you're being most impolite. Manners, P.P., manners. There's a gentleman at this table."

The man tossed me a quick "hi" over his shoulder. The Face wasn't accepting that as adequate.

"May I present Mr. Peters?" he said. "You won't believe this, but it's Mr. Paul Peters. It has to be that his father couldn't resist the initials. Mr. Peters, Mr. . . . ?"

"Bagby," I said.

For the moment The Face allowed himself to forget that he had been in the middle of an introduction. He came to a full stop.

"George Bagby?" he said.

I admitted it.

"Stick around," he said. "You're looking at a clown who has murder in his heart."

"It's a good place to keep it," I said.

"Spoken like a cop," The Face said, "but you are sort of a half cop, aren't you?"

Peters interrupted. "Look," he said, "I asked you to. You know I'll make it worth your while."

"You asked me to and I haven't," The Face said. "Since I asked you to get lost and you haven't, I'd say we're just about even up."

"I spend a lot of money in this dump of yours," Peters said.

"If you want me to love you, you could just mail it in."

"Why won't you?" Peters was nothing if not persistent. "Give me a reason. Why won't you?"

"Because they're big girls. In case you haven't noticed, they're the biggest. I hire them to get up there and strut. Beyond that they're on their own. For me they're just the Towers. If they want to follow on the rest of the line and get themselves burned, that's their lookout. I will have no part of that."

"You could tell me her name."

"If that's all you want, it's Cynthia," The Face said.

"Cyn," Peters said. "I like that—Cyn."

"And the wages thereof is death."

"Stop with the jokes."

"Who's joking?"

"I'll write her a note. Will you let one of the waiters take it back to her dressing room?"

"Her dressing room? They all of them dress together."

"You know what I mean."

"I know that I told you I'd give you her name if that was all you wanted. I should have known you'd want more. That's your type, never satisfied."

"What about it?"

"Get lost. I know I said that before, but at the risk of boring Mr. Bagby, I have to repeat myself."

"You said yourself they're on their own. So what's it to you if I send her a note?"

"I run a club. For the post office you go around the corner."

"You take my money," Peters said. "What do you think I come here for?"

"You're my most faithful fan?"

"The hell I am."

"Then it must be for tit elation."

There's never been a clown with more precise enunciation. The pun was unmistakable. It was wasted on Peters. The Face looked at his watch.

"It's coming up funny time again," he said. "Bring your drink along and come around back with me."

It was obvious that he was addressing this invitation only to me. Peters had no drink. Hastily the man tried to change that. He signaled the barman. Jocko had been waiting for it. The way he leaped into action, you would have thought that he had been crouched down in a sprinter's start. He tore into the concoction of something complicated.

The Face was on his feet. I got up on mine. Peters rose with us. It wasn't manners. He was coming along.

"You don't have a drink," The Face said.

"Jocko's making it right now. He can send it around back."

"Around back is work place. No drinking allowed."

"Him," Peters said, pointing to the glass in my hand.

"Special case. If I leave him here, he's stuck with you. There are things I won't do to a friend and that's most of them."

Peters, nothing if not single-minded, jumped at that.

"Leave him here and take me back with you," he said.

"No good. That way I'm stuck with you and that I don't do to me."

"She's back there."

"And you're out here. She has work to do. I've got rules. No johns in the working area."

"After the last show you'll see. You can't keep me out of the alley," Peters said.

"At your risk."

The Face planted the flat of his hand against the man's chest and shoved him back into his chair. At just that moment Jocko came rushing over with the drink he had elaborated for Peters. That one wasn't entrusted to a waiter. That one was served in person. It didn't look like a drink. It looked like a fruit salad strayed out of what used to be known as a women's magazine. (I have a decent respect for women, so I don't know what to call it.)

The Face linked his arm in mine.

"Let's go, George," he said. "All right if I call you George?"

"What do I call you?"

"People call me The Face."

"That how you sign your checks?"

"Banks have no sense of humor," he said, "but you're not a bank."

He led me backstage to his dressing room. It was unlike any other dressing room I had ever seen. It had the make-up table and the standard mirror ringed with light bulbs. It had the pegs on which hung his changes —an assortment of baggy pants and one pair of neatly creased slacks.

The rest of it, however, followed none of the conventions. There were books and none of them was Joe Miller. The collection seemed to be about evenly divided between poetry and porn. There was nothing wrong about his taste in poetry. In porn he appeared to be less discriminating. I looked at the books. That's habit. First thing in any room I look at the books. Inspector Schmidt says I do it in the hope of seeing some of mine.

In that dressing room, however, there was something

else and it quickly drew my attention away from the books. It was bits and pieces of architectural ornament. If that suggests anything tiny, forget it. These were great, heavy hunks—concrete cornice blocks elaborately molded, carved stone corbels, capitals. It was a great collection. Some of the pieces I could recognize. They had come off old buildings I'd known around the city. They brought back memories of facades that had given the city its individual look before they had been demolished and replaced with something that was as profitable as it was faceless.

"Do you give all the heavy spenders a rough time?" I asked.

The Face was doing minor repairs on his make-up. He wasn't wearing much, only enough to keep the stage lights from wiping him out.

"P.P.," he said, "is special. The Towers are big and they're built. To look at them, you'd think they could handle a guy and a marshmallow like P.P. easily."

"Can't they?"

"It has to be that he dazzles them with the dough, and somehow when they are not watching for it, he gets them at a disadvantage. His idea of fun is knocking women around and in my book 'around' is worse than 'up.'"

"A forewarned Tower," I said, "could have a go at knocking him around. It might teach him a lesson."

"Yeah, like picking girls his own size," The Face said. "Any one of the girls could and you'd think they would. The hitch is they're too stupid and too greedy. A C-note stuffed down the décolletage gives them the flutters. It maybe even anesthetizes them. So then they're wide open to a punch in the mouth."

"How does he reach that high?" I asked.

"Beats me," The Face said, "but he reaches. Before I knew about him, I let him get at one of them once. Phyllis—she's the one with the big smile. She didn't have all that much smile before but she was out of the show for weeks while a dentist was giving her the new front teeth. When I said a punch in the mouth, I wasn't talking any love taps."

"And he gets away with it? No assault charges?"

"He pays. He pays for the new teeth. I don't dock her for the time she can't work, but nobody tells him that. He pays her for the time. He throws in a fur coat to boot. He's big on fur coats. You ever heard what they say about the girls in apache dance acts? It hurts only until Saturday night."

"So it's worth it to them," I said.

"But not to me. I have no Saturday nights."

It was time for him to go onstage. He took me out to watch from the wings. The Towers went on first. As they gathered for their entrance, he pulled one of them out of the line.

"Mr. Bagby here," he said, "wants to see the smile."

She stopped and she smiled, giving me the full gleam of it. Something was evidently expected of me. I did my best.

"Beautiful," I said.

"The best smile money can buy," The Face said, as he sent the Towers strutting out to their audience.

"Which is Cynthia?" I asked.

"Number Two spot, second from the right end."

Since they were very much a matched set, I can't say that the girl in that Number Two spot looked any huskier than the others but then again she looked to be no less well muscled than the rest of them. She would be a lot of woman for Peters to handle but no more so than the one called Phyllis.

The show had been on for only a couple of minutes when another spectator joined me in the wings. It was a hunk of guy who looked as though he might have strayed out of an exhibit in the Museum of Natural History. His was a physical type generally believed to have gone out with the Neanderthals.

He was big, perhaps not exceptionally tall, but so big in all other dimensions that he seemed shorter than he was. If it weren't for the fact that collar sizes and hat sizes are based on different standards, his collar size and his hat size would have been identical. His neck was that thick. In shoulders, arms, and chest he was phenomenal and he tapered down to a slender waist. Slender for him, however, would have been enormous on you or me. It was only in relation to the mass of his shoulders and the volume of his chest that his waist looked small.

He had almost nothing you could call a forehead. His hairline seemed to rest on his eyebrows but in some inexplicable way I could see that he was scowling. How a man could manage that when he had no forehead to scowl with I don't know. It may have been, however, that the very fact of the scowl being concentrated in so small a space was what made his scowl carry such a heavy load of rage and menace. There was also his breathing. It was heavy and audible. It would be only a small exaggeration to say that he was snorting like an enraged bull.

It would have surprised me not at all if he had gone charging out on the stage to join the act. He looked as though he was holding himself on a tight rein and was in imminent danger of breaking out of it. He was sweating under the strain. I could smell it on him.

The Face came off briefly for a change of funny hats. Gargantua made a grab at him.

"He's out front," he said.

"So what else is new?" The Face said. "Isn't he always out front?"

"Always don't make it all right."

"Always makes it something you live with."

"One of these times . . ."

"One of these times you'll end up at the bottom of the river with the crabs feeding on your face."

"He don't scare me."

"He don't scare anybody. It's his army and you know it."

"You're always telling me that."

"You're always needing to be told. Either you don't listen or you don't remember."

"He better not go near her."

"He won't go near her. He's already been there."

"And I gotta go on holding still for it?"

"Relax. He's got his eye on someone else."

"How do I know?"

"Because I'm telling you."

By then The Face had switched the hats. He trotted back onstage. The behemoth turned to me.

"That sumbitch out front," he asked, "he after yours?"

"No," I said.

"You got to be sure. He's after one of the kids. It could be yours."

"No. He said Cynthia."

That was a mistake. I should have kept my mouth shut. I should have known nothing. Up to that point his eyes had been on the stage. He had been talking to me out of the side of his mouth. Now he gave up on watching the Towers to turn and look at me instead. It was a baleful look and with it his hands tightened into fists. The guy had enormous hands. As fists they looked like a pair of wrecking balls.

"He been telling you?" he said. "You buddy up with the sumbitch?"

"No," I said. "I heard him telling The Face. He's been working on The Face and getting nowhere."

That helped. The hands came unclenched.

"Yeah," he said. "The Face, he's okay."

"A funny man," I said. "A very funny man."

"Yeah, and a good guy. He's all heart."

Conversation seemed to be expected of me, and I could think of no place to take it from there.

"Which one is yours?" I asked just for something to say.

"Philly," he said. "You know. Phyllis."

"Lucky man," I said.

"Yeah. Not that they ain't all good kids. Which is yours?"

"Nobody," I said. "I just got talking to The Face and I came back here with him when he had to go on."

"So he's getting you fixed up. None of them you won't do okay with. You just don't get no ideas about Phyllis."

"I'm not getting any ideas about anyone," I said.

Again it was the wrong thing to say. We were immediately back with the baleful glare and the clenched fists. The guy was on a short fuse.

"What's the matter? They not good enough for you?"

"Hell, no," I said. "They're great. They're plenty

good enough for anybody. A man couldn't ask for
more. It's just that I like mine small. It's the way I am."

I had found almost the right thing to say. The fists
unclenched and the look went through a transforma-
tion. It shifted from menace to pity.

"The little babes," he said, "they're no fun. First
thing you know you're hurting them."

"I'm careful," I said.

"You can't have much fun being careful."

"I make out," I said. All the time I was asking myself
how I had let myself fall into this idiotic exchange.

"You watch the TV?" he asked.

"Not much," I said. "When I do, it's mostly sports."

"Like wrestling maybe?"

In talk with anyone else I would probably have
blurted out my opinion, but things were beginning to
be friendly and it seemed the better part of wisdom to
keep them that way. I refrained from saying that TV
wrestlers were phonies.

"Not much," I said. "I don't look at anything much.
Mostly I'm too busy for it."

"Rich Dawson," he said. "That's me. Rich Dawson."

"George Bagby," I said and I offered him my hand.

He took it, but not to shake. It happened so fast that
I have no way of telling you just what moves he made.
All I know is that he made them and there I was
enveloped in a wrestling hold. I don't even know what
it was called. It may have been a half nelson. It may
even have been a whole one. It felt at least that, but
it's an area in which I could hardly be more ignorant. I
just have a hunch that nelsons come only in halves.
Don't bother to tell me if I'm wrong.

I knew that a professional fighter is not permitted to
throw a punch unless it's in formal practice of his

sweet science. He loses his license if he does. I think he may even go to jail. Whether any similar prohibition is laid on professional wrestlers or whether they are free to pin anybody anywhere I don't know. I followed the prudent line. I said "uncle."

Laughing, my newfound friend converted the hold into a bear hug.

"You're okay, George," he said and turned me loose.

"You're that Rich Dawson," I said, as though I knew.

"Yeah," he said. "That's me. People watch me all the time and they don't know me without I got my clothes off and the oil on me."

"It does make a difference," I said.

"Next time you catch me, you'll see," he said.

"I'll be watching for you," I promised. "But now I'm going to pull out. Say good-night to The Face for me."

"Sure thing. See you, George."

"See you, Rich."

I moved back out front. I'd had all I could possibly have wanted of The Topless Towers. I was ready to be on my way. Peters was still out there, but now he was deep in talk with another man. I nodded in passing, but Peters wasn't leaving it at that. He made a grab at my arm.

"Bagby," he said. "Give me a sec."

I stopped, waiting for him to go on.

"Yes?" I said.

"I've written her a note. I thought maybe you'd take it back to her."

"What made you think that?"

CHAPTER 2

He said nothing. He just took a backward step. Simultaneously the man with whom he had been talking stepped forward. It could have been like folk dancing if the man hadn't grabbed a solid fistful of my coat, pullover, and shirt. With a jerk that fell just short of lifting me off my feet, he hauled me in close. We were all but chin to chin.

"Watch it, bud," he said. "You better watch it. You don't talk to Mr. Peters like that. Nobody talks to Mr. Peters like that."

"Now wait a minute," I said.

Peters was smiling. Can you fault a man for smiling at you? Under those circumstances I could.

"Henry here," Peters said, "is not a patient man. You can't expect him to wait long. For him a minute may be too long."

I tried talking to Peters past his goon. "There's a man backstage who's aching to take you apart," I said. "And don't think he couldn't do it—both you and this boy of yours, the two of you at once. So far The Face has been holding him off, but the guy is hair-trigger. It isn't just what will happen to you if you go back there. Just carrying your message will do it. Your messenger will be getting himself badly damaged."

Taking his cue from Peters or possibly just taking enjoyment on his own, Henry was also smiling.

"Bud," he said. "You're on the way to getting yours out here."

I was telling myself that this was crazy. I was telling myself that it couldn't just go on, not with all those people in the place. A quick glance at all those people, however, told me I was wrong. The checkroom girl, the waiters, the piano player, and all the customers were working hard at being unaware. The bartender alone was taking notice but he only to the extent of watching with another of those smiles of lewd enjoyment. I could have been a better show than the whole line of Towers.

Telling you what I did about it doesn't come easily. I'd like it a lot better if I could say I did something dashing and heroic or even that I stood up to it like a man and took whatever might have been coming. I can only plead that a man would have to be a fool not to recognize that he was standing alone and that he was hopelessly outgunned.

Henry was not of the dimensions of Rich Dawson, but there was no question of his being muscle and even less question of his being mean.

"I have no choice?" I asked.

"Henry doesn't give choices," Peters said.

"This guy backstage," I said. "Rich Dawson. It may be that it will be me first. But if it is, Peters, he'll just be warming up on me. He'll come out here after you."

"He'll have to get by me," Henry said.

He still had me in that grip, but he needed only one hand for it. With the other he dove into a shoulder holster and brought out a gun. Ramming it into my gut, he prodded here and there as though looking for a spot where he would be on target for a vital organ. I

know all that great stuff they tell you a man can do if
someone makes the mistake of pressing a gun muzzle
up against him. The recommended routine is a quick
pivot to bring the gun barrel parallel to you and a simultaneous sweep of your arm to knock the gun away.
Movements of body and arm are quicker than finger
movements, they say. If you are any good at it, you
should be clear before he can get his shot off, and in
the moment when he is dealing with the recoil of his
futile shot you're supposed to disarm him.

So I knew all that and I was aching to give it a try,
but that was as far as I could go. I could ache. I had
been told about it. I had seen demonstrations of it. I
had even practiced it with Inspector Schmidt. There
had even been an occasion when I had seen the inspector perform in just such a situation. He had been up
against a maniac. The man had been completely out of
control and he had been holding a gun pressed into
Schmitty's belly. The inspector had done it. He had
not only come away without a scratch, but he had
come out of it with the gun taken away from the loony
and the loony subdued.

When I had practiced it with the inspector, it had
worked beautifully for me; but it was like judo drill in
the army. You're working with a cooperative opponent;
everybody is being most careful not to hurt anyone
else. So there I was. I had no guarantee that I would
be any good at it. More than that, I was not in a rehearsed situation. Henry not only had the gun in my
gut, he had that solid grasp on me as well.

Belatedly I was remembering that I also knew how
to deal with that. You clamp your right hand over your
left wrist and bring your arms up in a quick, hard

thrust. I could have done that and broken his hold. It might have been at the cost of some torn clothes, but threads are only threads.

I knew all that, but the knowledge wasn't the first bit of good to me. I was in a spot in which neither of those moves brought off alone would suffice. I needed to make both of them. I couldn't go for the gun until I had first broken his hold. Until then I could neither do the necessary pivot nor make the move to take the gun away from Henry. By that time I would have taken a revolver slug in my gut. There was probably an approved way of dealing with the combination, but nobody had ever told me about it.

I did what I could. I resorted to guile.

"Okay," I said. "Give me the note, but don't say I didn't warn you."

Henry looked to Peters and Peters nodded. Henry returned the gun to the holster. I had been promising myself that if he did that first, I was going to permit myself the luxury of breaking his hold, but I didn't even get to apply that small ointment to my injured self-esteem. He made both of his moves together. While his one hand was taking his gun off me, his other was turning me loose.

I could see that he wasn't happy about it. But even as Henry's smile faded, Peters was broadening his. The man was now all childish glee and eager anticipation. He pushed his message into my hand. It was a fifty-dollar bill wrapped around a sliver of something stiff. It was fastened with an elastic band. I could guess that the bill was wrapped around a visiting card.

Plunging the hand that was holding his message into my pocket, I headed backstage. The show had finished by then. It had in fact finished just before Henry had put the grab on me. I hadn't the first idea of where to look for the dressing room where the Towers would be changing and I had even less thought of going there. Returning to The Face's dressing room, I barged in without knocking.

The Face was out of his baggy pants and was removing his make-up.

"You," he said. "Okay, George. Come in and shut the door. I thought you'd taken off."

I wasn't stopping for any explanations.

"Got a phone back here?" I asked.

"Booth out front," he said. "It only costs a dime."

"Not even that," I said. "Calls to the police are free."

"Police? You want to get me raided?"

"You want to get your place shot up?"

The Face sighed. "Don't tell me," he said. "It's Henry again."

"That's right. Henry."

"Pulling a gun?"

"On me."

The Face had been looking bored. Now he looked startled.

"On you? How come on you?"

I gave him a quick rundown.

"You've got the note?"

I brought it out of my pocket and dropped it on the make-up table. He slipped off the rubber band, unfolded the fifty, and set it aside. I had been right about the visiting card. The Face held it up to his nose.

"Only man in the world who carries perfumed cards," he said.

"Let's not horse around. I'm calling the police and I'll be bringing charges against the two of them."

"I wish you wouldn't. I wish you'd just leave it with me. Let me handle it."

"How are you going to handle it?" I asked. "Are you going to give the girl that card? I'm not holding still even for being a party to it."

The Face drew a cigarette out of a pack he had lying on his table. He lit it and then held one corner of the card in the flame of his cigarette lighter. The card caught fire. He held it till the flame came close to his fingers. Dropping the burning card into his ashtray, he watched it burn there till there was none of it left uncharred.

"That all?" I asked.

"All you need to know, George, my friend. That's just to tell you that you won't be a party to anything. There's no message to deliver. I didn't read it and now it's burned and nobody can read it. So you just take the fifty and I'll let you out through the alley."

"That's not funny," I said.

"Making funny? That I do only on stage. You don't want the fifty? Forget I suggested it. After all, you're right. It's Cynthia's. I'll give it to her."

"No good," I said.

"I know. You won't be a party to anything. So you won't be because there won't be anything. It's my fifty now and I'll give it to her and I'm not telling anyone where it came from. I've confiscated it. What I do with it now is on me."

"And you want me to drop the whole thing? No charges?"

"You can go out of here and call the cops," he said. "There's no way I can stop your doing that. I can only ask you not to. I can handle it. You bring the cops into it and it'll be trouble for me."

"Suppose you make the call yourself," I suggested.

"Still trouble for me. Peters pulls too much weight in too many places. Gang places. High places."

"You're playing with fire," I said.

The Face turned a pointed look at the charred card in the ashtray.

"Not anymore," he said. "It's burned out."

"Then I just go out through the alley and forget anything ever happened?" I said.

"If you will, I'll love you for it."

There was a small curtained window above his make-up mirror. He stood up and pushed the curtain aside, but only an inch.

"All right," I said. "How do I get to the alley?"

He dropped the curtain and came away from the window.

"You don't," he said. "You go out the front way, through the saloon. They've gone around to the alley. They'll want to know if you delivered the message and you won't want to lie to them."

"If they're out there, what will be with the girls?" I asked.

The Face chuckled. "Tonight everybody takes off through the saloon."

I pulled out of that backstage area and I had every intention of going straight on through to hit the street and head for home. Why I should have had second thoughts I'll never know. That I've never been able to explain it satisfactorily to Inspector Schmidt is the least of it. I've never been able to explain it to myself.

It had something to do with curiosity and something more with self-esteem. My move backstage had been humiliating. I suppose I was hoping to counteract that by putting a bit of swagger into my return. So much for the self-esteem factor. The curiosity?

I'd had two drinks from Jocko's hand. One had been mostly water and the other mostly whiskey. I was wondering whether, with The Face not on hand, he would go back to normal or if something lasting had been established in that department. I am not even certain that it wasn't simply that I wanted that other drink.

Whatever it might have been, I bellied up to the bar and ordered another of the same. I had expected that I would be watching the barman make it, but instead of doing his pouring out on the bar as he normally would, he took off into some back area where he was out of sight. When he returned he was bringing the drink with him. He set it down on the bar and shoved it toward me. I looked at it. I held it up to the light. It looked like a drink of the second order. It was quite brown enough.

I set it back on the bar. I was leaving it untouched.

"It's the way you want it, ain't it?" Jocko said. "It's like The Face told me."

"I like it mixed right out in front of me."

Jocko shook his head. "Can't do it," he said. "Not when it's like this, a special. Can't go mixing no specials out here where everybody can see. It'll be every guy he comes in here he'll be wanting them like this and even the way it is we have enough trouble with guys getting sloppy drunk. The Face says you get them like this. So maybe he knows you can handle it. Maybe he don't know nothing, but then that's his lookout. I'm just following orders. If it was up to me and you don't like the drinks the way I make them, I'd just bounce you out of here and you could go do your drinking someplace where you like it, but The Face, he calls the shots."

All of this was low-voiced and for all of it he was leaning forward across the bar. It was confidential stuff, for no ears but those of the specially favored patron, the friend of the management. I was being afforded a rare view into the inside workings of nightclub operations. All of the time, furthermore, Jocko had me fixed in an eye-to-eye confrontation and he was doing it with a half smile. There was challenge in that half smile. He was waiting for me to show him that I could take it.

"Let's have a drink together," I said. "You drink this one and let me watch you make mine."

He thought about that for a moment, but only for a moment. Then he was enlisting me in a small conspiracy. If I would just move down the bar a step or two, he could make the drink where I could watch the pouring, but I'd have my body screening what he did from the observation of some patrons farther along the bar.

That drink he made up right in front of my eyes. I watched his every move. It was much whiskey and no more than a touch of water. He pushed it along the bar to me and picked up the drink I'd rejected. He tossed it off in a linked series of swallows.

I picked up my glass and took a sip. Jocko kept me fixed with his eye and again he was smiling but what had been no more than a hint of mockery was now growing into open derision. That was part of it. The rest was the goon, Henry. He hadn't been in the place when I came back out to the bar. I had taken The Face's word for it that the lug had been out in the alley with Peters, but now he was back. I caught his reflection in the bar mirror and watched him lumber through the place to settle himself at the table nearest the door to the backstage area.

I took it as obvious that the guy had planted himself there with the intention of directing traffic. Anyone Peters wanted coming to him in the alley was going to be denied the alternative exit. That he was showing no interest in me I found astonishing. I would have expected him to come over to ask whether I had delivered the message.

That he didn't I could take to mean only that he was so completely confident of his own capacity for terrorization that it couldn't occur to him that there would have been any possibility that I might not have done exactly as I had been told.

I could see no likelihood but that things were about to get messy and uncomfortable. My own position in this developing situation was as absurd as it was unnecessary. The whole thing was no concern of mine and, whatever its outcome, there was no reason why it should affect me. If I was at all involved, it was only by a stupid accident. I had to be a fool not to take the simple course and uninvolve myself. The time had come for me to drink up and go home.

I was telling myself that what I was doing was no more nor less than good sense; but, underlying that judgment, I was having some thoughts of the ignominy of gutless flight. I tossed off the remainder of my drink in one ostentatious gulp. That was Bagby's gesture toward asserting his manhood.

I had thought of it as the requisite gesture. I had expected that it would serve to wipe that derisive grin off Jocko's ugly face. It didn't. I remember that and I

remember shoving money across the bar only to have it
shoved right back at me.

"The house bought that one," Jocko said.

I remember his words but at the time I was evidently past dealing with them. I was having other
problems. I had developed a wobble of the knees, a
rapidly increasing instability. It seemed to me that all
of the rest of me was in good shape, but in retrospect I
must admit that it was a delusion born of the fact that
the dysfunction wasn't limited to my knees. I know
now that I had it in my head as well.

You will probably agree with Inspector Schmidt in
his contention that in my head at least I had to have
been somewhat enfeebled when I'd first gone into the
place. That, however, is a matter of opinion and it has
little to do with the story I'm telling you.

I did get myself out to the street. It was at best a
staggering progress, but I made it. I have a clear memory of myself out there. I was at the curb, hailing cabs
and getting nowhere. It was not that there was any
lack of taxis. It was a clear night and the hour was late
enough to have been well past any rush time. Empty
after empty went whizzing past, ignoring my hail.

A young woman came along and offered a suggestion.

"You'll have to get up," she said. "You'll have to be
on your feet before any of them will stop for you."

I think it was not until she had spoken that I had
any realization of not being on my feet. Once she had
mentioned it, however, I did recognize that I was sitting on the sidewalk. At the time it didn't seem to me
that it was at all an odd thing I was doing. I wanted to
be off my feet and I was off my feet. It was as simple
as that.

"When I have a cab," I said, "I'll get up. Not before."

It was again an assertion of my manhood. I was not anyone who could be pushed around. Who were these cabbies to tell me whether I should stand or sit? I didn't feel like standing and I was going to do as I pleased.

She offered to help me up.

"I don't need any help."

"Then get up."

"I will. When I want to, I will."

"You can't just sit there."

"Who says I can't?"

That stopped her. It gave me the delusion that I was being brilliantly sharp and witty.

"I suppose you can if you like," she said, "but you do want a cab."

I drew myself up to my full height. It was, of course, just sitting height, but it gave me a great feeling of dignity and command.

"On my own terms," I said. "Not on theirs—only on my own terms."

"You're a nut," she said, "but a nice sort of nut. You're so nice that I'd like to take you home with me but you're so nutty that I won't."

I couldn't see where that demanded anything of me. It called for no response. I offered none. Instead I made another try at flagging down a cab. Again it was no good, but she hailed the next one that came by and it stopped.

"Here's your cab," she said. "So now get up."

I wasn't even going to try. I knew I couldn't make it and I seem to have been determined to accept no help.

"Not my cab," I said. "It's yours."

The cabbie took a hand. "That's right, miss," he said. "I take you. I don't take him. Drunks the likes of him I don't need."

"And I don't need a cab," she said.

"You hailed me."

"For him."

"No way. I'm not taking him. I don't. Never the likes of him."

"The two of us," she said. "I'll come along and I'll take care of him. He'll be no trouble."

Don't ask me why I should have resented her making promises for me, but at that point I did.

"I'll be all the trouble I want to be," I said, "and nobody's going to stop me."

"He's real nice, ain't he?" the cabbie said and pulled his cab away.

"You had to go and open your big mouth," she said.

"Nobody pushes me around."

It was ridiculous, of course, but I must have been possessed with compensating for my craven performance inside The Topless Towers. Overcompensation is always ridiculous.

"If I get you another cab, will you behave yourself?"

"No. Thank you very much, but thank you. No."

"You want to be left alone?"

"I won't let anyone push me around."

"You just want to go on sitting there?"

I may have made some sort of an answer to that. I don't know. I can't even vouch for the accuracy of these exchanges as I'm reporting them. For some time I had been drifting back and forth, going out of consciousness and making recurrent swings back in. Somewhere along in there it stopped. I went out and stayed out.

I report this part of it as what I remembered. The rest of it also seems like memory but with the difference that for this much of it my memory can be backed with independent corroboration. The rest of it is a pendulum swing between nothingness and nightmare. The nightmare aspects were peculiar in that they didn't terrify me. They had in them the ingredients for terror and for horror, but I remember that, even as I was experiencing them, I seemed to be comfortably aloof from them.

I suppose I should call it not nightmare but phantasmagoria. I cannot say I had no awareness of the horrors. I knew they were there and I knew I was the subject of them, but it was as though I might have been standing away from myself, a torpid and not too interested observer of what was happening to me.

The nightcap served to me on the house had been special, but not in the way that Jocko had indicated. It had been Jocko's own specialty and, as you know, I had been warned. The Face had told me that Jocko's mickeys were much admired. Jocko himself had drunk what I had expected would be the mickey. I had watched him pour my drink. How he had put it over I couldn't imagine.

I have no memory of being kicked, but the next day I was carrying the bruises that indicated as much. I think I can remember being dragged, but I could have reconstructed that from torn clothes and the fact that the curbside, which had been my last remembered resting place, was not the place where I was found sleeping off my mickey finn.

I had still been unconscious when I was taken to the

hospital, but later when I was told where I had been found, I was considerably less astonished than I might have been. I had these pictures in my mind and no way of knowing whether they might have been distorted memories of some moments of waking or phantasms that in a drugged sleep had been triggered by some actual discomfort.

I'd been found not in the street but in the alley that led to the stage door of The Topless Towers. It was the alley I hadn't used because Peters and his Henry had been posted out there and an encounter with them had been contraindicated. Then, however, Henry hadn't been out there all that long since I had seen him back in the saloon while I had been downing that special drink I'd watched Jocko make me.

I had assumed then that Peters had been standing watch at the alley door alone. I knew I hadn't been back there with him. On waking, however, I was told that I had been. I'd been found lying in the alley with Paul Peters. That he might also have been slipped a mickey seemed reasonable enough. I could well imagine The Face ordering one up for him.

I could, however, make no sense of The Face having ordered one up for me. Our relationship had been amiable from the outset and it had remained that way. We had parted friends. It was far easier to believe that my mickey had been Jocko's idea, all his without an assist from anyone. That, however, left me wondering about Peters. A similar special for him could hardly have been Jocko's idea. I had too vivid an image of Jocko as a pleased and eager recipient of the Peters largesse.

There was also the question of why anyone should have gone to no small trouble to bring the two of us together. I tried to think that in some moment of waking

I might have had the half-sane impulse to hide myself away from that too conspicuous public position at curbside. I might then have walked or crawled away into the relative seclusion of the alley. There were, however, the tears in my clothes. They indicated strongly that I had been dragged. If not into the alley, then dragged where and to what purpose?

It was all most unsettling and I didn't need the concluding bit. That was a cop bending over me and demanding that I explain why I had been holding, grasped in my hand, a shattered segment of dragon's tail.

That in my drugged sleep I might have seen dragons could have been suitable even to the point of cliché, but I had no memory of having seen any. That this police officer might have invented one with which to taunt me defied belief. Invention wasn't the man's style. He would have gone for the established joke—the pink elephant.

Everything was coming at me in jagged and incoherent segments. There was nothing that I could fit together with anything else. I could recognize that I had been in the alley or at least in an alley. I remembered pavement stretching from wall to wall, innocent of curb or gutter. I remembered lying in some kind of sticky gook. I had been curious about that but I'd been in no shape to make the effort it might have taken to identify it.

I was told that Peters had been there with me, but I had no way of verifying that. I hadn't seen Peters. I'd seen a pulpy red mess that didn't look like anyone. The whole business was too confusing. I couldn't begin to cope with it. Furthermore I had nothing I could bring to the coping. Lethargy seemed to be all that I had to offer. I could see no profit in trying to rouse myself.

If I stayed awake, people would be making demands of me and they would be unreasonable people with unreasonable demands. There was that cop with his nonsense about a shattered hunk of dragon's tail. Certainly a police officer who was seeing things like that would have to be a cop in trouble. It may have been that I was unsympathetic, but I think I told myself that it was his problem and I wasn't going to let him bother me with it.

So it may have been a deliberate act or it may have been no more than a surrender to the inevitable. I removed myself from all the problems. I went back to sleep.

That, of course, couldn't go on forever. The time came when I woke and, like it or not, no more sleep was possible. I didn't like it. There was one of those throbbing headaches that makes you feel your head has grown to twice its normal size and for no reason but that nothing smaller could contain so large a bundle of pain.

I was in a hospital bed and that seemed extreme. For a hangover headache it was clearly excessive. The hospital room, furthermore, was unlike any I had previously occupied. Its window was barred. Its door stood ajar but the doorway was also barred and just outside it sat a cop. He was no cop I knew. Through my association with Inspector Schmidt my acquaintanceship in the department is extensive, but it can hardly extend to every last patrolman on the force.

My relations with all the cops I've known have always been the friendliest and that had always been

equally true with cops newly met. I had no reason to
expect that this lad was going to be different.

"Hi," I said. "I have a couple of questions."

The cop got up and looked at me through the bars.

"Before you ask them, mister," he said, "and before
you say anything more, I got to read you your rights."

"You can skip that," I said.

"You can shut up and listen, mister. You're not telling me what I can skip and not skip."

"I know my rights," I said.

"So you're one of them. Then maybe you know the
law doesn't say you have to know them. It says I have
to read them to you. Maybe you're a lawyer. Maybe
you're even the Chief Justice of the United States
Supreme Court. It makes no difference. You get yourself arrested and I've got to read them to you like
you're maybe a guy who never even learned to read."

This then would be a cop who worked by the book,
except that there's nothing in the book that would
have told him to be surly about it. I waited with my
questions while he read me my rights. When he had
finished, I did my asking. They were the obvious questions. I wanted to know where I was and why I was
there.

"Bellevue," he said. "Prison ward and you're here till
they'll be ready to take you out for arraignment."

"Arraignment? On what charge?"

"How do you like homicide, mister?"

"I want to make a phone call."

"Like I told you, you can call your lawyer. It's your
right."

"I'm making my call to Inspector Schmidt," I said.

"Inspector Schmidt, is it? Inspector Schmidt's a busy
man. Inspector Schmidt takes over on the tough cases.

Inspector Schmidt can't be bothered when it's open-and-shut. He has no time for your kind—you got yourself caught red-handed."

"There have been times and not a few of them," I said, "when the inspector has looked at what some dumb cop has called open-and-shut and has seen that it's all wide open."

"You calling me a dumb cop?"

"I'm making my phone call to the inspector."

"Are you now, mister? How would you like a slap in the mouth?"

"How would you like a departmental trial?"

CHAPTER 3

It was, of course, just a lot of chitchat. He had no choice but to take me to the phone and let me make my call. It isn't often that I can't get right through to the inspector. He can be tied up—closeted with the Commissioner or some such—but then there had always been the message taken and the message expeditiously delivered. There had always been an explanation and apology and the promise that Inspector Schmidt would be getting right back to me.

This time, however, it was different and so different that it convinced me that I did need my lawyer. The inspector wasn't available. There was no knowing when he would be free. He would be given my message, but I wasn't to count on his calling me back.

"Inspector Schmidt makes it a practice to ignore calls made to him by persons in detention. He prefers not to interfere in the orderly processes of the department. If there is anything in your case that requires his attention, it will come to him in due course."

"Are you kidding?" I said. "Who am I talking to?"

I thought I knew the voice, but I couldn't believe it. There wasn't a man among Schmitty's boys whom I hadn't been calling a friend. By the sound of the voice I would have been certain I had Jerry Quinn, but I was telling myself that I had to be mistaken. None of the inspector's people would ever be taking that tone with me and least of all Jerry. I had known the guy ever since he had first made detective and first been assigned to the inspector's Homicide force. I had been at his wedding. Inspector Schmidt had been best man, but I had been there.

"Your call is on record. Your message will reach the inspector in due course."

"Do you have the name right? George Bagby."

The character had it. He spelled it for me.

"You know who I am?"

"You are in detention awaiting arraignment."

"I am George Bagby in detention awaiting arraignment."

"Inspector Schmidt makes no exceptions, Mr. Bagby."

And that was it. He hung up on me.

All through the call my surly guard had been just about on top of me. Although he had been hearing only my end of it, there had been enough in that to occasion in him a large measure of sadistic joy.

"Okay, Mr. Bignoise Bagby. You've had your call."

"Not to my lawyer."

"That's your lookout. You've had your call."

He couldn't deny me my right to call my lawyer, but he could give me a hard time about it and he did. I insisted and, after much argument, I got to make the call. Jeff was out of his office, and the response I had from his secretary was all too much like what I'd had on the call to Inspector Schmidt. She didn't know how soon he would be in touch. Pending that, she didn't know where she could reach him. She would get my message to him as soon as she possibly could. She left me with the impression that she wasn't going to be putting any sweat into it.

So then the cop moved me back to that barred hospital room. There was no need for him to prod me along with pokes of his billy club, but he indulged himself. It was nothing much, nothing that would put even a minor mark on me. It was just a humiliation. Along with it he kept urging me to try to give him some trouble. He was all but begging me for an opportunity to beat me into submission.

The day had come to be something that was an extension of the night, just another level of nightmare. I tried to tell myself that it wasn't happening, that I was still asleep, that I was going through nothing more than some more dreams.

The morning wore away. Noontime brought me a tray, but before my guard passed it in to me, he removed from it all the cutlery. Since it was that plastic stuff that cuts nothing, the removal clearly had no reasonable purpose. It was simple harassment. Watching me eat with my fingers was going to amuse him.

I disappointed the guy. Hangover headache plus my predicament served to erase all appetite. I had no interest in food. Also I can't say that there was anything on the tray that offered temptation. I drank the brew that passed for coffee and left the rest.

By midafternoon I was alternating between trying to recall how long a man could be held before the law required that he be arraigned and wondering how long a tour my guard could be working.

It was midafternoon when Inspector Schmidt turned up and then he just stood there appraising me coldly through the bars. I waited for him to say something. He didn't.

I had to be the first to speak. "What the hell goes on?" I asked.

The inspector ignored the question. In fact, he made a great show of ignoring me. Turning his back on me, he talked with the cop.

"Has he been behaving himself?" he asked. "Been giving you any trouble?"

"No trouble, Inspector," the cop said. "Nothing I couldn't handle. It's just he's been uppity. He thinks he's something special."

"You read him his rights?"

"He wasn't much interested. He thinks he's got more rights than other people."

"Okay," Schmitty said. "Open up. I'm going in."

The cop unlocked the bars. Once the inspector was inside, he locked them behind him. Schmitty looked me over.

"You have heard your rights," he said. "You have the right to remain silent and anything you say can be used against you. You're in trouble, bad trouble. If you level with me, I'll try to do my best for you, but it's your decision whether you want to talk to me or not."

"I want to know what all this crap is about," I said.

"It's about you. It's about your thinking you can do any crazy thing comes into your head and count on me to come running over to get you special treatment and haul you out of it. When it's been little things, I could handle it for you; but when it's homicide there are no special favors."

"When did I ever ask for special favors?"

"Today. You've been yelling for them today."

"Because some dumb cop got everything wrong and put me here? I never killed anybody and you know damn well I didn't."

"How do I know?"

"Because you know me."

"That means nothing."

"All right. My mistake. I thought it meant a lot."

"Okay," the inspector said. "Suppose you tell me where the dumb cop went wrong."

"I had a stupid night," I said. "I got fed a mickey. I woke up here. I don't have to tell you about mickeys. They put a man out of action. They don't make him go berserk."

"Somebody went berserk. Who?"

"You guys are talking homicide," I said. "So somebody killed someone. Isn't that it?"

"It is, but it doesn't have to be berserk," the inspector said. "It can be deliberate. It can be done in cold blood and that's the way this one looks."

"Which makes it Bagby, the deliberate, cold-blooded killer?"

"You were there and there's a piece of the murder weapon big enough to work for fingerprints. It took great prints and all of them are yours."

"Hold up a minute," I said. There was something there that woke an echo. In the light of the total picture it might have been a trifle, but to me it loomed so large that I had to have the answer to it. I was convinced that my sanity hung on it. "A piece of the murder weapon? What the hell kind of murder weapon comes in pieces?"

"It was dropped on the guy and it killed him. Hitting the pavement, it shattered. It damaged the pavement as well. It was one hell of an impact. So most of it is in smithereens, just the one sizable piece of it left."

"Sizable piece of what?"

"The tail."

"Tail of what? Don't say a dragon."

"Why not a dragon?"

"Because I'd rather not think I'm going crazy."

"What do you know about this dragon?"

He was asking the question and asking it seriously. If it hadn't been that I had the memory of that cop hassling me about a dragon, I would have thought it was the inspector who had lost his mind. As it was, I had to think I was losing mine. I answered him and I guess my answer was a reach for sanity.

"This dragon," I said. "Any dragon. It's a mythical creature. Dragons don't exist except in fairy tales and religious metaphor. St. George killed one."

"That's the one they say it is," Schmitty said.

"With my fingerprints on its tail? Come on!"

"You better start from the top and tell me everything about last night," Schmitty said.

"I just told you. It was a stupid night and I got fed a mickey. You tell me about the damn dragon."

I did want that but I also wanted a little time to think about the mickey before I answered the inspector's question. The thing had been poured right there in front of me. Except for its effect on me, I would have no evidence for calling it a mickey. Searching my memory, I could think of nothing I might with reason hold against The Face.

I had taken a liking to that extraordinary little guy, and I could see no way that he might have ordered up a mickey for me. The way I was reading it, it had to have been a mickey and it had to be the bartender pulling that one off on his own, getting something of his own back for having been humiliated before me. I wanted to think that it would be something that I could take up with The Face or that I could even handle it one on one with his man, Jocko. I was thinking that I didn't want to have any part in anything that could bring about the closing down of The Topless Towers.

You must understand me. Part of it was my liking for The Face and part of it was that it seemed fun to have a Kit Marlowe nightclub around. I suppose I should have been taking my predicament more seriously but at that point the whole thing seemed too ridiculous. The Topless Towers was good for laughs. A man doesn't find many things that good for laughs.

"A big, heavy hunk of stone," the inspector was saying. "It happens it was carved in the shape of a dragon. It could have been any of the other things they carve out of stone—an angel, an eagle, Justice, Liberty, Civic Virtue, anything they carve in stone. So it happens it was a dragon or just the tail end of it. Dropped from the roof on a guy down below, it's a killer. The guy is pulped and he's dead."

It was a relief and it wasn't. Having the thing lifted out of the hallucination department had to make me more comfortable in my mind. That, however, was the only thing I could pull out of it that even resembled a plus. A piece of a dragon's tail with my fingerprints on it had been the stuff of madness. Except insofar as it shook my confidence in my sanity, I had been seeing it as nothing to which I would ever need to give serious consideration.

This, however, was something else again. It was too neat a fit to at least one of the things I remembered of my crazy night. There was The Face's collection of carved and molded architectural ornaments salvaged from demolished buildings. I couldn't remember seeing a dragon in the man's dressing room, but in that jumble of cornice blocks, corbels, pinnacles, grotesques, and what-have-you there might well have been some segment of a stone dragon I had overlooked.

I also couldn't know whether I had seen the whole of the collection. There could have been much more of it in other parts of the backstage area. I hadn't seen everything back there. There was the room in which the Towers dressed. I could well imagine that there were storerooms as well. There would have to be a place where liquor stocks were kept.

"Who?" I asked.

"A guy named Peters. Paul Peters, do you know him?"

"Not what you'd call knowing," I said. "We were introduced last night."

"Since when do you know that kind of people?"

"I just told you I didn't know him. We were only introduced." I couldn't quite leave it like that. I made a try at filling out the picture. "Immediately he tried to presume on the introduction. He wanted me to do him a favor. He even pressured me. I didn't do it."

"We'll come to that," the inspector said. "First who introduced you?"

"I don't know the man's name, only his stage name."

"Okay. His stage name, what's that?"

"The Face."

"Simon Drew. That's his right name. You were in that dump of his? Witnesses say you were. I've been hoping they were mistaken—that or lying."

I've already told you of Inspector Schmidt's refusal to understand the lure that pulled me off the street and into The Topless Towers. I'm not bothering you with any of that again. Let's leave it that I did what the inspector had asked at the outset. I gave him the full account of my crazy night, all of it—what I remembered clearly and all of that area of confusion in which I couldn't separate nightmare from fact. Just as he had pinned down to fact the maddest part of it all—the dragon's tail—he also cleared the fog from some of the rest of it.

Like all the other restaurants and nightclubs in the city, The Topless Towers was not served for the collection of its garbage by the city's Department of Sanitation. Commercial food establishments do not rate such service at the expense of the taxpayers. They contract with private truckers to cart their refuse away.

The truckers do the rounds of the city between three and six in the morning. That schedule has them on the streets during the lightest traffic hours and it makes it possible for them to hit even the latest-running places after closing time.

It had been five-thirty when the collection truck had pulled up at the head of the alley that led to the service door of The Topless Towers.

"The way these collection guys tell it," the inspector said, "they almost pulled away without picking up anything. The way it looked from the head of the alley, the whole area back there was strewn with garbage. It's their job to pick up the bagged stuff. They're not paid to clean up any scattered mess. What they were seeing, of course, was all that broken-up stone—that and blood."

The inspector continued with the statement the truckers had made. They'd decided to go in and pick up whatever refuse there might be that they found properly bagged and intended to leave the rest of it.

"As soon as they started in there, they saw right off that they weren't about to touch anything," the inspector said. "They found you lying there in the middle of the mess. They thought you were dead and why not? You were out cold and lying in a pool of blood. You were sharing the blood with Peters and anybody could see that he was dead. They got themselves out of the alley quick. They were out at the curb puking when they flagged down a passing squad car."

"Right," I said. "So a dumb cop out of the squad car finds me there. I'm passed out cold in the dead man's blood and I've got my hand on the hunk of dragon's tail. He decides real quick that I was up on the roof with a dragon and I dumped the tail on Peters. Then I went down to the alley to make sure Peters was dead. By that time, exhausted by so much exertion, I just lay down in my victim's blood and went sleepy-by. I can understand that. It isn't easy, but I can understand it."

"Well, that's something," the inspector said.

"It isn't much," I said. "What I can't understand is that the dumb cop's idiotic scenario seems to have been holding up all day and holding up even with you. I don't expect you to take any special view of the thing just because you know me. I do expect you to take one look at anything this ridiculous and kick it away on sight. I've known you to do that again and again when the suspect was nobody you knew and the story you rejected was one hell of a lot more plausible."

"That cop wasn't as dumb as you think," the inspector said. "He was mistaken but that can happen to any of us anytime. He's a young kid. He lacks experience. He didn't dream up any nonsense like your going up on the roof to drop the thing on Peters and then going down to see whether you had killed him. The way he saw it, you and Peters fought in the alley. You picked up the hunk of stone and brought it down on the crumb's head and killed him."

"It's still dumb," I said. "I then lay down beside him and went to sleep in his blood?"

"You'd been fighting. Peters had you just this side of knocked out. You worked up one last surge of strength and just before you passed out yourself you beaned him with the stone."

"You can believe that?"

"No. Not on the evidence. It would take someone superstrong—a weightlifter type—to pick up a stone that heavy and bring it down on a man's head. Even then, although it could kill the man, it would be something like a skull fracture. It wouldn't mash him. For that it had to be the stone dropped from the roof."

"And that," I said, "brings us back to the even stupider scenario. More than that, I'm here. The doctors must have looked me over. That's part of the evidence, too. Haven't the doctors told you I was in a drugged sleep? I was sleeping off the mickey."

"That's part of the evidence, too," the inspector agreed, "but they have no way of determining whether you had the mickey before Peters was killed or after. They can't tell us anything on that."

"I see," I said. "So the story is I killed Peters and worked out an elaborate cover-up. I fixed myself a mickey, drank it down, and went out to the alley to sleep it off. It was a mild winter night, but it was winter. It could just as well not have stayed mild. Out in that alley I could have died of exposure, but I would have been too stupid to think of that possibility. I would do all that, so that even when the evidence stacks up against me like those fingerprints, I can say I was framed. Wouldn't it have been a lot simpler just to wear gloves? It's the season for gloves. Isn't it obvious that I was fed a mickey and, when I passed out, I was dragged to the alley and left there with my hand carefully rested on the dragon's tail so it would have my fingerprints on it?"

"Exactly," Inspector Schmidt said. "It's been expected that would be your story."

"My story? After all, you know me. Can you believe that other of me?"

"No, Baggy. I have no story. I didn't buy that other one for a minute, but that's only me."

"You're Chief of Homicide."

"And your friend. That's going to make it rough. I'm your friend and everybody knows it. That's bad and what makes it worse is that this is one that has everyone watching. Paul Peters was well connected. He had all kinds of connections and only some of them were gang connections. There's going to be a lot of pressure. There already has been and it's only the beginning. Big people are interested and those big people are yelling for your hide."

"You're my friend? I haven't been noticing much in the way of friendliness today."

"Baggy, you dope. Haven't you tumbled that it's all been an act? It's been a necessary act. I have to play it that I'm out to nail you. I'm mad because you thought you could use me to get you out of anything, even murder. It has to look as though I have this personal interest in nailing you because otherwise this Peters murder is going to be taken out of my hands. We came close to that this morning."

"You sure you haven't been overreacting?" I asked.

"I know what you're thinking," the inspector said. "It's Jeff."

Jeff, I have to tell you, is more than my lawyer. He's an old friend. We were friends at college and we've been close ever since. How close? I'm godfather to Jeff Jr.

"Yes. What about Jeff? Why did you have to get him into the act? Do those big people of yours say I don't have a right to counsel?"

"Look, kid," Schmitty said. "You must trust me. I needed the time. You get through to Jeff, then there'd be no way to explain his not moving and moving fast. He'd have had you out on bail before I could even get my act going. Now when he gets you out, all those big shots will be satisfied that I gave you a hard time. I was real unfriendly. That will hold them for a little and we need the time."

I dropped my voice. "Aren't you giving yourself away?" I asked. "Your man out there is all ears."

Schmitty didn't join me in any whispering.

"That's Johnny," he said. "I picked him for this. I picked him because he's a good man and a good actor."

I was thinking that Johnny might have been overacting, but I let it pass. It wasn't important.

"So besides me, who was he acting for?"

"Anyone," Schmitty said. "No one. There was no way of knowing. When there's this much heat on, there can always be somebody who'll be reporting."

"So much heat," I said. "This Peters bastard had friends in high places and they are out to get somebody. Okay. But what makes it Get Bagby Week?"

"You've been set up to be the prime suspect. Drew says he did everything he could to keep you out of the alley. He can't understand what could have made you go in there. Everybody and his uncle—bartender, waiters, checkroom chick, piano pounder—they all say that right out there in the barroom you tangled with Peters and you came out the loser. Nobody knows anything about a mickey but everybody says you didn't get it there. The bartender tells it that you demanded extra-strength drinks. He also says he poured your drinks right before your eyes. He says he could see you were taking on more whiskey than you could handle."

"He poured the last one right before me," I said, "but only the last one. He's a liar. The one before that may have been the mickey."

Since I had already given Schmitty my account of the evening, he knew the timetable.

"No," he said. "That wouldn't do it. They're not that slow-acting. What is possible is that you saw him pour it and what did you see? You saw him pour stuff that looked right and out of a bottle that looked right. Suppose it was a bottle that behind its all-right label was filled with premixed mickeys. It looks to me like a real cute operation. He gives you a drink you have every right to suspect and, of course, you turn it back. He pours you another where you can see and adds on the convincer. He drinks down the one you wouldn't touch."

"I told you he was a liar."

"Understandably. He won't be admitting he slipped you a mickey. No bartender ever would even when there's nothing like murder involved. What about the rest of them and what they're saying? All lying?"

"By omission," I said. "Truth maybe, but not the whole truth. The Face did send me out the front way."

"His name is Drew," Schmitty said.

"The other is easier to remember."

"Yeah, I know. Because of the Marlowe lug, but his name is Simon Drew."

"Okay. Drew saw that Peters and his thug had moved out to the alley. He wanted to get me away from there without any trouble."

"He thought you might make trouble?"

"Is that what he's saying?" I asked.

"He's not saying one way or the other. He leaves it open. He tried to keep you and Peters apart, and if you hadn't gone into the alley, you would have been kept apart. That's all he's saying."

"But the obvious implication is that since I ended up in the alley, I must have gone there looking for trouble. Right?"

"That's the inference that's been made."

"And nobody's telling any of the rest of it, like I was passed out on the street out front and in no shape for getting from there to anywhere else on my own. I couldn't move. It has to be that someone moved me. Some of these people at least must have seen me out there and seen the shape I was in. The whole truth would have included that."

"They're frightened people," the inspector said. "The thing comes too close to them. So as a suspect they like you fine. You're an outsider and you're all they have to take the heat off them."

"But this garbage they've been piling up against me," I protested. "There's no way it can be fitted together even to begin to make sense."

"But you're George Bagby. You're the guy who would know how to fix it so that it would look that way."

"What?"

"Think of it as a compliment," Schmitty said. "Sure enough, it is a compliment of sorts. And not only to you, but to the both of us. You're in the story-writing business and the stories you write are murder stories. So, comes the day you have a murder to commit, you know all the ways there are for getting the trail so tangled up and muddied that nobody will ever be able to pin anything on you."

"Yeah," I said. "And you?"

"I have the detecting skills. You and I are close. I can be expected to use all those skills of mine in the interest of not detecting. What you haven't already tangled and muddied they are expecting I will. So they'll have to be watching me carefully."

"Peters was a creep," I said. "According to The Face . . ."

Schmitty interrupted. "Drew," he said.

"All right. Drew. According to Drew, he was a sadist as well as a creep. The town must be full of people with motives for murdering him and they'll be motives far better than mine."

"Yours? You're not saying you had a motive, any motive, good or bad?"

"Detached disapproval," I said, "if you want to call that a motive."

"I don't," the inspector said, "and you don't either. You don't want to be saying things like that, not even just as a way of talking."

"All your big shots that are leaning on you, Schmitty, don't they know that Peters was a creep?"

"They're being careful not to say it. You tell me Drew called him The Golden Creep. He sure was that, always big at election time. Nobody bigger with the campaign contributions. Campaign after campaign, he bought himself a lot of gratitude. In return he got away with a lot. The slammers are overcrowded with better men. So it wasn't that he hadn't always been collecting some sort of payoff, but now it seems to be the time of the big payoff and you have to put yourself in there. You'd be a lot better off never having heard of this Marlowe guy."

"We've been over all that," I said. "You mean Peters had everybody bought?"

"The people that count, at least enough of the people who count. The ones who have the clout. The ones who are in office."

"He was that good at picking winners?"

The inspector shrugged.

"With the kind of money he'd pour into a man's campaign," he said, "how could anybody lose? In an election, if you can spare no expense, you're a shoo-in."

"But there are election laws. There's a limit on the amount a man can contribute to a candidate."

"There are ways," the inspector said. "Peters had the dough and the pols know the ways."

CHAPTER 4

Since such was the beginning, my position in this investigation was unlike what it customarily had been. I was not just the detached observer preparing to do an account of the case. I was a participant central to the investigation. It had taken skill, diplomacy, and all that playacting on which I have already filled you in for Schmitty to get me moved even that far off dead center.

I was no longer the prime suspect, but I did remain a suspect. Whether I was to be seen as a suspect who was cooperating eagerly with the inspector in an effort to get at the truth or one who was cooperating with the inspector even more eagerly on a collaboration that would further muddy and confuse the trail of guilt depended on each man's will to believe and on which view of the matter he might choose to exercise that will.

The difficulty of the situation was immeasurably increased by the too many people who would have been best suited by having the thing kept quick and simple. Bagby would be the murderer and the case would be closed. To these people it was important for the investigation to shut down before it could turn up anything about what Paul Peters had been or just who had been the beneficiaries of what he had been.

"As I told you," Schmitty said, "Drew and all his people in that lousy club will go along with putting it on you because any other way they are probably involved and, if nothing else, it may be bad for business."

"But they are involved," I said. "Peters was there. I was there. It was there I was fed the mickey. Peters was waiting at their back door when he was killed. They can work their tails off to involve me, but how can they possibly be thinking that they aren't going to be involved along with me?"

"Desperation. They know where they stand and they are making a desperate try at getting out from under. They can't, of course, but getting the heat on you, they hope, will take a little of it off them."

"I wouldn't have expected it of The Face," I said. "He seemed like a nice little guy."

"Drew? A nice little guy? What made him seem like that? Just because you and he go for the same poet?"

"Yes. That was at least a part of it. It made him a touch more civilized than you'd expect in a dump like that."

"Like civilized enough to get a customer bumped off with a knife in the tavern instead of smashing him out in the alley?"

"That was a long time ago," I said, "when life was rougher."

"Rougher than when?" Schmitty asked. "Surely not now."

"Anyhow the way Christopher Marlowe died, if he did die that way—you can forget about that. It was all over and done with centuries before any of us were born."

"Unless it tells me something about the way Drew's mind works. That's important since he's not at all a bad candidate for the prime suspect spot."

I had to demur. I can't pretend that I was too noble to do what everyone else seemed to be doing—having a try at playing the any-suspect-but-me game. My problem was that I couldn't see any way where putting the heat on The Face could do anything much for me.

"Drew was contemptuous of Peters," I said. "He was laughing in the guy's face. It's too big a jump from that to killing a man. If anything, I would have thought it could go the other way."

"Peters killing Drew?"

It seemed a bit extreme, but I was telling myself that we were confronted with extremes.

"Peters would have delegated it," I said. "He had a goon with him. He called the guy Henry. Henry packed a gun and he held it on me."

Schmitty had already had full details on that, but now he wanted a description of Henry. He picked up quickly on my description.

"Hank Lusk," he said. "I didn't know anybody ever called him Henry unless maybe it was his mother. But Peters bringing Hank into the act—that will take some thinking about."

"I wouldn't put anything past that one," I said, "but isn't it the wrong victim for him? He was Peters' man. Also lifting heavy weights when all he had to lift was a gun? Would that be his style?"

"It might be," Schmitty said, "but there's a more promising way of looking at it. Peters brings Hank into Drew's saloon. He doesn't travel with Hank because he likes Lusk's company. Hank comes along as a threat. As it happened, the threat was used on you, but Hank hadn't been brought along for that. Nobody knew you were going to be there. You didn't know it yourself until you had the silly impulse to walk in. Hank was there in case it became necessary to lean on Drew. That's Hank's line of work."

"But he didn't on Drew," I said. "I was the one."

"You first, but what's to say Hank couldn't take two in one evening? So if Drew got leaned on or he felt it coming on and moved to forestall it, he could have decided he could spare the dragon's tail out of his collection."

"It was in his collection?"

That seemed a stupid question but I asked it anyhow.

"He says not. He says he wanted it, but it was too expensive. He says if he had stretched a point and put out for it, he would have taken good care of it. He says there are plenty of cheap items in his collection, stuff he can even duplicate. It didn't need to be anything as good as that dragon. Some minor piece would have done the job. The way he talked about it, he could have been thinking the dragon's tail was a far greater loss than Peters."

"If it was Drew and he was eliminating a threat," I said, "wouldn't his target have been Henry and not Peters? Henry is the threat. Peters was a cream puff."

"There would always be more Henrys where Hank comes from, and Peters could buy them by the dozen. They're just as much on the market as the politicians, and they come a lot cheaper."

"That thing must have weighed but plenty," I said.

"Falling feathers don't smash skulls."

"Getting it up to the roof to drop it from there. That took muscle."

"More muscle than you have?"

"Up five flights of stairs? You're not kidding."

"Also more muscle than Drew has," Schmitty said.

I did some thinking aloud. "Rich Dawson," I said.

"The wrestler? He has it that you were after one of the show girls and Peters was queering your act."

"He was the one with the itch to get his hands on Peters," I said.

The inspector sighed. "But that's like all the rest of it —your word against his, your word against Jocko's."

"What about his muscle against mine?" I asked.

"You could have managed it. Drew could have managed it. Anyone could have managed it. There's an elevator."

"You'd have to know it was there and where to find it."

"Not necessarily. You were in Drew's dressing room."

"I saw no elevator."

"You saw the collection he had in the dressing room."

"I did."

"Any St. Georges? Any dragons? Even any pieces of one or the other like a dragon's tail?"

"I didn't see any."

"If there had been anything like that, wouldn't you have seen it and taken notice?"

"Very likely. I was interested in the things."

"Did you know that what you saw in the dressing room is only part of the collection?"

"No. I just saw what was there."

"Drew could see you were interested?"

"We talked about the things. My interest was more than perfunctory. I'm sure it showed."

"He didn't tell you he had a lot more of it upstairs, even a lot of it up on the roof? He didn't invite you to go up and have a look?"

"Is he saying I went upstairs?"

"No, but you didn't see any dragons in the dressing room and he says it wasn't his. He couldn't afford it. A collector meets a guy who's interested in his collection. Doesn't he jump at the chance of showing it off, all of it?"

"A lot of the time he'll be showing it off to people who aren't even interested," I said. "But it was time for his second show. He was about to go on."

"It could have been that and it could have been that he had a reason for acting like he wasn't a collector," Schmitty said. "He didn't want you going up where you could see his expensive prize. He didn't want you seeing it because he had plans for it."

"Then," I said, "you're thinking The Face and not Rich Dawson, the muscle?"

"I'm thinking everybody," Schmitty said. "All of them and the Towers, too. Those are hefty dames. They pack plenty of muscle. For now I'm keeping an open mind."

"Can I hope it's not so open that it can include me?"

"No, kid. Not that open. Not with so many people working so hard to put it on you. On that alone you'd have to be in the clear."

As far as it went, that was great, but I wasn't going to be happy until the inspector came up with a lot more. A lot more came and it was without either he or I doing anything to bring it in. It came from Ethel Cameron and she turned up quite of her own accord to volunteer it.

By that time I had been turned loose. Schmitty had

given it the pitch that he had examined the evidence carefully and had been unable to find anything on which I could be held.

He was way out on a limb doing even that, but he had put on a good act during those first hours and he had a considerable assist from the doctors at Bellevue. Their findings supported my story. They had seen and had recorded the evidence of my having been fed a mickey.

So I was turned loose. I was a free man, but I can't say I had been freed from suspicion. The tabloid rags and the TV people were going to town. Any murder can be news, but for a killing to be big news it needs that something extra.

If a prominent or notorious person is involved, that will do it. If the circumstances of the killing are sufficiently bizarre, that will do it. So for the news guys the Peters killing had everything. It was MILLIONAIRE PLAYBOY MURDERED. It was FRIEND OF THE GREAT SLAIN. It was CRUSHED BY A DRAGON'S TAIL.

It was also CRIME WRITER AT THE SCENE. It was even CRIME WRITER SLEEPS IN DEAD PLAYBOY'S BLOOD. Without accusing this "crime writer" of anything, the total of what was reported came to something like "Bagby says these things. Everyone else with any knowledge of the affair contradicts him."

It might have been a feeling that they were skirting too close to the edge of libel that made them so assiduous in overworking the word "alleged," but it was piled on to such excess that it gave my every quoted statement a spurious ring. At best I seemed to be represented as a necrophilic ghoul. At worst I was shown in the guise of a sinister character, a brain dangerously equipped with all the skills and devices requisite for killing and getting away with it.

I was back home and alone. I had looked at all the papers and I had caught the TV coverage. I was trying to dismiss all that as par for the course, but I was having no marked success with doing it. There was the telephone. It must have been the SLEEPS IN DEAD PLAYBOY'S BLOOD bit that stirred the sludge in what seemed to be every sick mind in town and even in some who made their calls long-distance.

There were denunciations and threats of divine punishment, but even the maddest of those were preferable to the invitations. There appeared to be a wide range of differing opinion on where I might be positioned along the sadomasochist spectrum. I was offered entrée to all manner of orgies, Walpurgisnachts, Witches' Sabbaths, and black masses.

The doorbell was a change from the telephone, but when I went to the door, I had my moment of doubt. My visitor was a gleaming vision of mauve satin breasts and buttocks. No satin has ever had more shine to it. It amounted to something like an unearthly glow. There wasn't much of the satin, little more than it took to provide a tight sheathing to each of the body's hemispherical protuberances.

Not all of those, furthermore, were completely encased. The neckline plunged, descending to depths at which bosom was not more than one-third wrapped. The short, tight skirt was slit well up the thigh. The earrings dangled. The eyelashes jutted. The perfume overwhelmed.

"I suppose you don't remember me," she said.

"Sorry. I don't. You must have the wrong address."

"No," she said. "This is right. I remember you."

"Then you have the advantage of me, Miss . . ."

"Cameron, but call me Ethel."

"What can I do for you, Miss Cameron?"

"Nothing for me, Georgie," she said. "It's what I can do for you."

I didn't know how to take that. It carried the odor of insult, but there was neither mockery nor malice in the way she said it. There was nothing of coquetry either.

"You'll have to jog my memory," I said.

"I didn't expect you to remember me. You can't remember anything about last night, can you? Sitting on the sidewalk? Remember that?"

"You tried to get me a cab," I said.

It wasn't any wild stab in the dark. By inches and by pounds she fell short of the dimensions that could have qualified her for a place in the line of Topless Towers. That left only the hatcheck girl, some feminine patron I could hardly have failed to notice, and the woman who had tried to help me snag a cab. I remembered the hatcheck girl as being on the small side. Ethel Cameron fell between a Tower and the checkroom chick. The chick was also a brassy blonde. Ethel was a coppery redhead, equally metallic but of a conspicuously different hue.

"I should have tried for an ambulance," she said. "What they're telling. It just ain't true."

Belatedly I asked her in and offered her a drink. She was in no hurry to accept. First she wandered through my apartment, looking at everything and admiring everything.

"You live nice," she said. "You live real nice."

It occurred to me that she could have been casing the joint, but I put the thought aside as unworthy.

"About a drink," I said.

"You got white wine?"

"Not cold."

"That's okay. With an ice cube in it."

I wasn't going to do that. A man has to draw the line somewhere. I had a better idea. In celebration of my homecoming I had opened champagne. The inspector had joined me in knocking off a bottle, but it has never been his drink and I'd found myself up to considerably less than I'd expected. I hadn't been completely recovered from the aftereffects of the mickey. For the time alcohol in any form had lost much of its lure. I had iced more than the one bottle.

"Champagne," I said.

"What I mean," she said, "just plain white wine."

"Champagne is white."

For a moment she smiled. It was a rueful smile. I thought I could see some pain in it. Ethel, however, was a cheerful type. The smile broadened to a grin and then she giggled.

"You know," she said, "it was maybe a million times I ordered champagne and I never once got any."

"So this time you didn't order it," I said.

My way of opening the wine disappointed her. In gleeful anticipation of the big pop she had clapped her hands over her ears. If in the opening process you have a napkin-wrapped bottle that isn't warmed by your hand, twisting it gently and firmly will ease the cork out. In that way you don't get the bang, but you don't get wine sprayed all over the place either.

She took a sip, scowled, and tried another.

"It tickles your nose and it don't taste of lemon," she said.

"Why should it taste of lemon? It's made of grapes."

"It always tasted of lemon," she said. "I knew it wasn't champagne, but it was supposed to be like champagne except that it didn't cost like that."

The wine grew on her. She took to assuring me that her first comments on it had not been made as criticism. She took to reminiscing. It had been back in her teens. In those days she had worked dance halls. There was nothing new in what she was telling me. It was the well-known racket.

The men bought dance tickets and took their choice of the girls. The girl collected a ticket for each dance, earning for herself a small percentage of the cost of the ticket. For a bigger profit she had to bring her man to a table between dances. House rules required that she order champagne. She was served some sweet fizz, which as she had said tasted of lemon, while the man paid for champagne. The price he paid should have brought Dom Pérignon. The girl got her small percentage of the profit, but in that department even a small percentage came to what Ethel called "a nice piece of change."

"It was good while it lasted," she said. "The lindy killed it. It had to be the waltz and the fox-trot—them kind of slow dances—to make it work. The guys they held still for the champagne, it wasn't they didn't know they was being took. It was they had ideas that maybe they could be buying something else. They had these ideas for you know what. Doing the lindy, they left whatever they had on the dance floor. They was too tired for having any ideas."

She was no teenager, but she wasn't a Gray Panther either. She was many decades short of that.

"Waltzes and fox-trots," I said. "They were before your time. You're not nearly that old."

"Yeah," she said. "You're a kid working the dance halls. The men, they're no kids. They're like fat, foolish, and fifty. For them it was the waltzes and the fox-trots. The young guys were lindying, but nobody was caring. Off the young guys nobody could make a buck."

"Then what happened to the older men?" I asked.

"They got older and older. If it wasn't they passed on, it was they just got sat down in wheelchairs. So there was the new fat fifties, but they was all overage lindy-hoppers. By then the kids were rocking. A girl had to quit that racket before it got so she wasn't eating. That's when I begun what I'm doing now."

I didn't ask what she was doing now. I had no need to ask, and it had become clear that her visit was in no way professional. She had come as a friend. Questions, it seemed to me, could have been taken as unfriendly.

"I have to apologize for not recognizing you right off," I said. "I wasn't making much sense that first time we met."

"You can say that again."

"I didn't even know whether I had really met you or only dreamed you," I said.

"You didn't dream me. I thought you was just looped, but I did wonder how anybody could get himself that looped."

"If a bartender wants to do it to you, it's easy. I got mine from an expert."

"I wouldn't know about that. All I know is you was looped." She seemed to be in a great hurry to get that in. Her tone carried an urgency that told me that not knowing was for her the least of it. She didn't want to know. It appeared to be important to her that she not know. "You were too far gone to get up off of the sidewalk. You never made it anyplace away from where you was. Not on your own, you didn't. You didn't move. You was moved."

"Did you see it?" I asked.

"I seen you. You was passed out on the sidewalk. You was passed out like dead."

"That's not what I meant. Did you see me being moved?"

"How would I have seen that?"

"You were around. You just might have."

"I wasn't around all of the time."

She had much to tell and it was all in my favor. What troubled me was the feeling she gave me, the feeling that there was more and that she was holding it back. I would have preferred complete candor. Looking at what she was giving me, I was wishing that I could have the rest of it. What that rest might have been I had no way of knowing. I didn't even know whether the whole of what she might have told could have been helpful to me or not. Out of misjudged kindness she could have been holding back on telling even me anything that she thought might be damaging to me.

She was not in the least reticent about her profession. She was completely open about the fact that she had been out on the street soliciting. The street in front of The Topless Towers was in her territory. That block and a couple to the north of it and another to the south made up her regular beat. Night after night she patrolled it. From her first sight of me she'd had no interest in me as a prospect.

"The way you was," she said, "any girl who would have taken you home would have to be one of them they roll drunks. There wasn't nothing else could be done with you and I'm not one of them."

"I remember," I said. "You tried. You wanted to do your best for me and I was no help."

"You was past being any help and you was way past it when that other bird was still alive."

"Peters?"

"Yes. Him got himself killed."

"You saw him?"

"You won't remember when I came back to you," she said.

"I remember when you were trying to get a cab to stop and take me."

"That was at first. I couldn't get you up on your feet and no cabbie was going to take you while you was down on the sidewalk. I kept trying but I wasn't doing you no good and I wasn't doing myself no good neither."

She had left me where I was and had resumed her cruising. Passing the head of the alley, she had seen Peters in there and had started up the alley to talk to him.

"When I got in there and seen who he was, I turned right around and come out again. I wanted me no part of that one."

"Why? Had anything happened to him? Was there something even then?"

"There was him. I knew about him. When a guy's like that, the word gets around. The man was crazy. He was mean crazy. He'd been hanging around that club a long time. So he was around there a lot, just about in the middle of the stretch I work. I could have had him anytime. That'd be anytime I had a big itch for going to the hospital."

"But you saw him in the alley? On his feet? Okay?"

"That's right. I seen him."

"You were saying you came back to me."

"It wasn't a great night. I walked down and I done myself no good. I was walking back to see how it would be up above. You was still where you had been but you was asleep, dead to the world, not like before when you was sitting there trying for the cabs. I went on past you."

She had done better on the northern stretch of her beat. She didn't go into details. She refrained not through reticence. It was just that who and where and what could have been in no way relevant to my predicament. I could guess that it had been a quickie since she said it was three quarters of an hour to an hour before she was again back at that spot out front of The Topless Towers where I lay passed out on the sidewalk. I was still there then, she said.

"You was like dead, but I knew you wasn't," she said. "You was snoring. I could hear you maybe a half a block away. I went on past you but not far, only to the alley. I went in there."

"The alley? You wanted no part of Peters."

"Him? I was figuring he'd been long ago gone from there. I was going to be a Girl Scout."

The good deed she'd had in mind had been to get me off the street. Passed out where I was, I was on display for anyone who might come by. It may have been that she had an idea that I was bad for business. She said nothing of that. She had just been hoping she could do me a kindness.

"I knew it wasn't no good my trying to take you home," she said. "You'd have to be carried or at least dragged and I knew I couldn't drag you that far. Crossing streets, down off the curb and back up again on the other side—I'd be ending up having to leave you in the gutter where you could maybe get run over even. The way I remembered it, going into the alley, it was going to be all level."

Before she had embarked on an attempt that might not have been feasible, she had gone into the alley to explore the possibility that she might be able to drag me in there.

"I didn't go far in there before I was slipping in the blood and stuff. It was too dark in there to see anything, but I struck a match and had a look. The only way I could know who it was, it was by that fur coat of his. The way he was then, he wasn't looking like anybody."

"It was after?"

"Maybe right after," she said. "Yes. Right after."

"How do you know that?"

"The blood was still wet. It don't stay that wet for long, does it? It begins to get thick-like."

I was still on my first glass of champagne and toying with it. She wasn't toying with hers. I kept pouring for her.

"You saw it and you didn't call the cops?" I asked.

"Me call the cops? Me when it was him?"

"Why not you?"

"Every reason why not. People been saying all along that it was going to be that one day some girl was going to turn on the louse and she'd squash him like you squash a louse. So how was I going to look? I'm a girl, and there he was, squashed like a louse."

I could have said something about the absurdity of

guilt through a figure of speech but, confronted with the absurdities of the stuff that had been stacked up against me, I was in no position to be scornful.

She had gone into a panic. She had gone back to where I was lying in my stupor and had made another attempt at rousing me, thinking that if she could wake me and get me on my feet, she might somehow get me away from there.

"Into the alley?" I asked.

"What do you take me for? I was scared silly, but not that silly. I'd have to be crazy even to go back in there. Drag you in there? How can you think a thing like that?"

"I can't," I said.

Rousing me had been hopeless and she had had to get herself away from there. She'd left me and just taken off.

CHAPTER 5

I made a try at moving back to a couple of the areas
where I had sensed what might have been spots of reticence, but it got me nowhere.

"I'm going to ask you to repeat all this for the cops,"
I said. "You know. Make a signed and sworn statement."

"Do I have to? I don't want anything with cops."

"Why not?"

"Cops. You know how they are."

"I do know. Cops are all right."

"Says you. You never been a girl, she's on the street."

"Not just any cop," I said. "Inspector Schmidt. I can
promise you. You talk to him. You tell him what you've
been telling me. You make a statement and you sign it
and swear to it, and you'll make yourself a friend."

"Inspector Schmidt? He's the one they're saying he's
your friend."

"Yes, and he'll be yours. He's a good friend to have."

"I don't know. I don't think I can."

"You came here to help me. Just telling it to me,
that's no help."

"Can't you just tell him?"

"It won't be the same thing."

The last of the champagne was still in the bottle. I
poured it into her glass. It was a diversion. While she
was busy with the wine, I rang the inspector and fixed

it up with him for me to bring her down. When I came away from the phone, her glass was empty. I took it out of her hand.

"You'll like the inspector," I said.

"It was him on the phone?"

"Yes. I called him."

"You told him about me? You told him who I was?"

"I had to. It's my neck and it can't do you any harm."

"I hope." She heaved a great sigh as she got to her feet. "Okay, George," she said. "Here goes nothing."

"You won't be sorry, Ethel," I said.

"Maybe not. I need the brownie points, I guess."

I got her going before she might change her mind. I'd had some parking luck that day. My car was at the curb. I'd caught the spot right in front of my door. She reacted to the car as she had to my apartment. While I was putting her into it, she was inspecting it and telling me how nice it was. As I was coming around to my side, I noticed a man across the street. He was lounging against a lamppost.

He looked familiar. Another time I would probably have lingered at least a moment or two in an effort to bring in the recognition. Just then, however, I had not even the first moment's thought of doing that. I was fixed on just one thing, getting Ethel Cameron to the inspector as quickly as possible. I could think of nothing then but the fragility of her acquiescence.

If I had kept the whole of my mind on it, I probably would have had it made in short order, but I had too many other preoccupations. There was the job of maneuvering through traffic for the speediest possible run down to Police Plaza. I had made the run too often not to know the route that was likely to offer the best possibilities, but even there I was not having the streets to myself. In New York there are no such streets.

Such attention as I could spare from coping with the traffic I was giving to keeping up a line of what I hoped would be relaxing chatter. I felt I had to keep Ethel from having second thoughts. Even though I was having the delusion that the seemingly familiar figure had gone out of my mind, some part of me must, nevertheless, have been occupied with it. In any case suddenly and out of nowhere the recognition came to me.

The loiterer I had seen across from my front door was Jocko. Dressed for the street, complete with overcoat, hat, and muffler, he had, of course, looked different from the way I'd been remembering him in his bartender's conventional white shirt with the conventional bow tie and the shirtsleeves rolled up tight above the bulge of the biceps. If I had been asked to describe the man, I would have been able to offer nothing much more than the Donald Duck tattoo he had on his beefy left forearm. It was an enraged duck. I had been remembering it as neatly representative of the man's temper.

Out in the street and dressed for the weather, he'd not, of course, had the enraged Donald on display. I would have been at a loss to say what there had been about the man that had brought me the recognition, but once it had come to me, I had no doubt. It was Jocko I had seen.

I wondered what he had been doing out there. I could only think that he had come to tell me something and had been loitering while he'd been whipping himself up to do it. In the light of the treatment I was convinced I'd had at his hands the night of the murder and the things he'd been saying since, I could well imagine him needing time for bringing himself around to the point where he could make himself step up and ring my doorbell.

I could see no possibility of anything but that he'd had a change of heart. I was only wondering at it and trying to imagine some mysterious agency through which such a miracle could have occurred. I was regretting that it had been impossible for me to stop with him. I was thinking that he wouldn't wait, that before I could get back home, some hard-won resolution would have been dissipated. He would have changed his mind and gone off. I thought that the first chance I had I might go around to The Topless Towers to see him instead of waiting on the chance that he would return to see me. I decided that it was not so much something to think about as it would be something I'd have to take up with Inspector Schmidt.

I kept telling myself that it had been a choice of risks. If I had recognized him at once and I had stopped for him, I would have risked losing Ethel Cameron. As it was, I was risking the loss of Jocko. I was telling myself that I had made the better choice. She was, after all, a bird in the hand.

Even though at the last it was a bit sticky, I did get her up to Inspector Schmidt's office. All the way down in the car she had been fine. She liked the ride. It was a new experience for her. On her own she used taxis, but she said that taxis were different.

"Guys," she said. "They drive in from Jersey or Connecticut or from Westchester where they've got the wife and kids. They cruise along in their cars and they pick a girl up, but it's only to ride the couple of blocks to her place. It's not like this. It's different. You're different. You keep both your hands on the wheel."

"In this traffic," I said, "I need both of them on the wheel."

"Yeah, but even if you didn't, you're different. You're a gentleman."

Down at Police Plaza, however, she went quiet. When I gave her a hand out of the car, I could feel she was shaking. I guided her in through the lobby and wished that the cop at the lobby desk had left it without greeting me. I hurried her past in the hope that she wouldn't notice his knowing smirk. I was remembering what she'd said about the way cops are. The last thing she could have needed was a demonstration. She did take notice.

"Cops," she said when we were in the elevator, "when they aren't mean, they're smart-ass. Most of the time they are going to be both."

"They're people," I said. "You have all kinds."

"Maybe but I ain't met up with any of the other kind."

"You're about to," I said.

Schmitty didn't let me down. He was at least as good as my word. He was warm. He was sympathetic. He was respectful. He was even courtly. She lapped it up. It stood out all over her. Given the first opportunity, she would be ready to tell him he was different, he was a gentleman.

She made her statement. With the inspector's questions to guide her, she did it smoothly and coherently. By the time she was approaching the end of it, she was so comfortably in gear that it was pouring out of her. Part of it certainly was that the inspector had made her feel so comfortable about what she was doing.

Along with that, however, it was not unlikely that
the time had come when the champagne was taking
effect. When she had been telling me her story, there
had been those touches of wariness. Those wore off,
but it was only at the very end that it came to anything more than a change in tone. What she was saying had come to carry a new sound of completely open
candor. At the finish, however, she did add something
that she hadn't previously given me.

The item that she added, furthermore, was no trifle.
In telling me her story, she'd said that after making her
last attempt to rouse me, she had given up on all
efforts to move me away from the murder scene and
had lost no time before taking herself away.

When, in making her statement for the inspector,
she came to that place in her story, she went into
greater particulars. She explained that when she left
me it had been with the decision that she was going to
call it a night. To have gone on patrolling her territory
had become impossible. It would have kept her too
much in the vicinity of the alley and she was having
none of that.

"I was packing it in," she said. "I was going home. I
live near there. It's only a couple of blocks but it's
downtown from there. Walking that way, I'd be going
past the alley again and I'd had enough of the alley
and of him and the blood and all. I didn't even want to
go past it."

She said that she crossed the avenue to go south on
the other side.

"I hated leaving Mr. Bagby where he was." We had
been Ethel and George or even Georgie, but in the inspector's office it had gone to a more formal footing.
"Across the street," she said, "before I took off, I looked

back. I guess I was thinking I'd maybe see him move or something and I could go back and try again to get him up off of the sidewalk, but then I saw I didn't have to."

Having gone that far, she suddenly thought better of what she was saying. She stopped short. After a moment of stammering hesitation, she took a grip on herself and tried to finish her statement.

"I took off and went home," she said.

The inspector wasn't leaving it at that.

"Let's back up a minute, Miss Cameron," he said. "What did you see that told you that you didn't have to go back to Bagby and try again?"

"The way he looked," she said. "He was sleeping. He even looked comfortable there on the sidewalk. He had that cashmere sweater on under the tweed jacket. It wasn't a cold night. He was nice and warm. It wasn't like he was going to catch pneumonia or like that."

"That was the way he looked when you were right there with him." The probing was gentle, but the inspector was probing. "What was different when you looked back from across the avenue?"

"Nothing was different. He was still sleeping. So I didn't have to go back."

"When you looked back, you expected he wouldn't still be sleeping?"

"Not really," she said. "But you know how it is. You get to thinking maybe I was too quick. Maybe if I waited just another minute."

That there was something more was obvious. She had been determined to give just so much and no more, but she had slipped. What we'd had from her was to the good since it gave strong backing to my own story, but it stopped there. Beyond establishing the most welcome time sequence, essentially it offered nothing new. On her evidence I had been out cold well before Paul Peters had been done to death by dragon tail. I liked that. I wasn't about to knock it, but, nevertheless, I was right in there with the inspector. I also wanted more.

Since we were convinced that there was more, just the simple fact that she was holding out on it made it loom large. Having already volunteered so much, she wouldn't be holding out on any trifle. The inspector told her that she was spoiling everything. She was reducing her very good statement to worthlessness.

"When you've got the truth," the inspector said, "but it's easy to see that it isn't the whole truth, you're not going to be able to make anybody believe that any of it is true. Everything becomes suspect. People get to thinking that you have some interest other than bringing out the facts. You lose your credibility as a witness."

I had some misgivings about the way he was putting it to her. I was thinking that he should have kept it much simpler. I was wondering whether Ethel Cameron would understand a word like "credibility."

She did understand it. She began to open up.

"I did see something," she admitted, "but it was such a little thing, not enough to do anybody any good. If anything, it'll maybe be bad for George."

"The truth could never hurt me, Ethel," I said, trying to cash in on the return to informality and hoping that I wasn't sounding too sententious.

She took a deep breath. I suppose resolution can't be built without a greater than normal oxygen intake.

"I saw somebody," she said. "Somebody was over

there looking after George. He wasn't going to be left the whole night sleeping in the street."

"I wasn't," I said. "At least part of the night I was left sleeping in the alley."

I drew a scowl from the inspector. I should have realized that the last thing he would have wanted at that juncture was an interruption. I clammed up. My interruption, however, seemed to do no damage.

"I didn't know it was going to be like that," she said. "I thought you'd be the rest of the night inside."

"Exactly what did you see?" the inspector asked.

"He wasn't down on the sidewalk anymore," she said. "Somebody had picked him up. He was being carried. He was slung over somebody's shoulder. You know, held by the legs with his head and his arms hanging down behind."

I was at the edge of breaking in to question that. I was ready to tell her that I hadn't been carried. I had been dragged. My ruined jacket and slacks attested to it. I opened my mouth to speak but I promptly closed it, biting back the words. The inspector wanted no interruptions. He knew about my clothes. If he wanted that brought up, he would do it.

"He was getting carried inside," she said. "It wasn't into the alley. It was inside."

"Inside where?" the inspector asked.

"There. Into the bar."

"The Topless Towers?"

"Yeah. In there. That's where he was. Right along there The Topless Towers, it's the only place."

"You saw him carried inside. Who was carrying him?"

"I don't know."

"Nobody you knew?"

"Who would I know?"

"You know the neighborhood. You're around there all the time. There must be a lot of the locals you can recognize when you see them."

"If locals go looking for pickups," she said, retreating into the wisdom of her trade, "they don't go looking right there around where they live or they work. They go someplace else to do their looking. People I could recognize, it's them they come in from Jersey or Connecticut or Long Island or like that."

"Men?"

"Of course, men."

"It was a man you saw?"

"A man, a woman, I don't know. It was across the avenue and it was quick, just maybe a second before they was inside and the door closed. It wasn't near enough or time enough for recognizing anybody."

"You recognized George."

"No, I didn't. It was more like I knew right off it had to be George. There was the place he'd been laying on the sidewalk. There was nobody laying there anymore. He was the one—he wasn't moving. He had to be carried. So there it was a guy being carried and George not where he was anymore. That ain't recognizing, is it? It's just knowing it had to be George. It couldn't be anybody else."

"Fair enough," Schmitty said. "But did you notice anything about the person who was carrying him? Do you remember anything?"

Before he had finished his question, she was already shaking her head. The inspector persisted.

"Big or little, fat or thin, tall or short?"

"Big enough to be carrying him," she said.

"Easily or was it a struggle?"

"I don't know. I wasn't near enough and it was too quick. I wouldn't know."

The inspector doesn't give up without trying. He went on working at it but, whether she had no more to give or she had found herself a cutoff point she sensed would not be damaging to her credibility, she was not to be moved.

The time came when the inspector sent the stenographer off to type up the statement for her signature. The waiting time was passed in chitchat.

Inspector Schmidt has no taste for small talk. I have never known him to indulge in it idly. In a situation such as this, however, where he feels it's demanded, he handles it as expertly as does any habitué of the cocktail circuit. He has a talent for it that seems none the worse for going long periods without being honed.

There was still that one point in her story that he had left unquestioned and it seemed as though he was about to leave it unquestioned. I was trying to tell myself that he knew what he was about, that if he was leaving it, it would have to be that it was not of such great consequence as I was attaching to it. I was ready to believe that; but, consequential or not, it was bugging me. I had to ask. Listening to their chatter, I could tell myself that I was interrupting nothing.

"Sometime during the night somebody kicked hell out of me," I said. "And sometime during the night someone had me lying flat on my back and took me by the ankles and dragged me across a floor or pavement or something. The back of my jacket shows it. The seat of my pants shows it. Both of them are torn and ripped at the back. They're a total loss. I've also got the bruises to tell me where I took a flock of kicks."

She made no comment on the bruises. "Oh, gee," she said. "That nice tweed jacket. It's a shame." Her regret seemed heartfelt and sincere, but then she brightened. She was determined to look on the happier side of things. "But with his blood and all on it," she said, "even if it could have been gotten out, you probably wouldn't have wanted to wear it anymore anyway. I know I wouldn't. My shoes, where I stepped in the blood, I didn't even try to clean them off. I threw them away."

"But you say you saw me being carried," I said.

"Like I told you. I said what I saw."

Her tone was unnecessarily vehement. It seemed so to me but I was left wondering whether I could have imagined it. I could see no reason why on that small point she should have been lying.

The stenographer returned with the typed-up statement. Ethel was ready to sign it without reading it, but the inspector slowed her down. He read it with her. She made only one comment before signing it.

"I don't talk good," she said. "I don't talk grammar."

"Who does?" the inspector said.

After the signing he told her that we would drive her back uptown. We would be seeing her home.

"No," she said. "No, thanks. I'll be all right. I'll take a taxi."

"The way taxis cost today," Schmitty said. "We'll be going your way anyhow. It'll be no trouble."

"It's only money," she said. "Cabbies, they got to live, too."

"Cabs aren't easy to find down around here," I said.

"Even if you're up on your feet and you're not hailing them from a seat on the sidewalk," Schmitty added.

She let herself be persuaded, but it was more as though she had been overruled. Although she tried to come along with good grace, it wasn't the same as it had been on the ride downtown. It was just the two of us in the car again. Since the inspector was going to be wanting his own car, he didn't come along with us in mine. He followed, driving his own.

She was tense and preoccupied. I thought she might have been regretting having come to me with her volunteered information. It was obvious that she had done that much without any expectation that she would be going to the police or putting herself on record with a sworn statement. She had also slipped into telling more than she had intended. That could have been worrying her.

I suppose for my part I was also preoccupied. I had one nagging question and I couldn't rid myself of it. That bit she had slipped up on, the one small item she had obviously planned on holding back, had me baffled.

I could find nothing in it that should have made her so reluctant to reveal it. I kept asking myself if it could have been what she had actually seen. I was inclined to believe that it was not. To me it smelled of a quick fabrication whipped up to cover her slip.

She had given me an address, and I had taken it without thought; but then, when I had begun watching the house numbers and realized that I was checking them prematurely, I found that I had something to think about. In her statement she had explained crossing the avenue before starting off for home by saying that she had been squeamish about starting downtown without crossing because then she would have passed the mouth of the alley and she couldn't bring herself to go back even that close.

The house number she had given me, however, was not downtown from The Topless Towers. It was north of the club. Expecting it to be south of the Towers, I had begun watching the house numbers while we were still too far downtown.

I said nothing. I had caught the discrepancy. I was thinking that it was something that was so obvious to me, it would be something Inspector Schmidt could not possibly be missing. I was leaving it for him to deal with it. I was expecting that he would speed up to pass me and that, when I would reach the address she had given me, he would be there ahead of us and ready with his question. He had heard her give me the address.

He didn't pass me. He appeared to be content with following along and I began thinking the impossible. He wasn't catching it. He had to be slipping.

I pulled up at the address she had given me. The house was more or less like the one where I have my apartment. It was a handsome old New York townhouse that had been cut up into flats. I was well aware that there were women in Ethel's profession who have achieved a high degree of affluence and who live in considerable luxury. Those, however, are the call girls. They work by appointment only. The place had too great a look of affluence. It was difficult to believe that it would not have been beyond the means of a girl who worked the streets.

"This it?" I asked.

"Thanks for the ride," she said.

She was losing no time about getting out of the car. Earlier she had been taking evident enjoyment from having me open the car door for her and helping her in, and it had delighted her when I had come around to open her car door for her and help her out of the car. Now she was waiting for no such courtesies. She opened the door for herself and was out of the car and across the sidewalk before I was out from behind the wheel.

The inspector pulled up right behind me. She was on the doorstep with her finger on a bell. The inspector started toward her but, without so much as a backward glance in his direction, she pushed the door open and hurried inside. The door locked behind her.

"She crossed the avenue because she had to go downtown to go home," I said.

"So," the inspector said, "if she wasn't lying about that, it may be that she doesn't want us to know where she lives. It can also be that she didn't want the neighbors seeing that she keeps bad company."

There were name cards on all the bells. None of the names was Cameron. The inspector had his notebook out of his pocket and he was copying off all the names. I had an opportunity to be helpful.

"The bell she rang," I said, "was second from the top."

"MacPherson," Schmitty said.

"Cameron and MacPherson," I said. "I can almost hear the bagpipes."

"She's about as Scotch as what the old-timers told me off-the-boat scotch whisky used to be during Prohibition. The same probably goes for MacPherson."

"So how good is her statement?" I asked. "How much can we believe?"

"All of it or pretty much all of it. What she put in is credible enough. The question is what she left out."

"She saw me carried into the club," I said. "I don't believe that."

"You think you're too heavy to carry? A strong man could do it or even one of those Tower babes. When you went into that dump, you walked into a den of muscle."

"She saw me being dragged into the alley," I said, "and she took off because that was something she wanted to be clear of."

"And then she came to visit you today? No way in the world you can make that work, kid."

"Then what?"

As always, Inspector Schmidt was seeing possibilities and he was keeping all of them open.

"There's nothing to say it's impossible for her to have seen you being carried into the club," he said.

"Why does a guy who can carry me then turn around and drag me?"

"Nothing to say it was the same guy. Why would someone who wanted you out in the alley carry you into the club?"

"He wanted me off the street," I said. "A cop could have come along and found me. Stopping to deal with me, the cop would be out of his squad car and much too close to the alley. There was a danger he would find the body before somebody was ready to let it be found."

"Not bad thinking," the inspector said. "First order of business then would have been to get you out of sight."

He explored the various possibilities for me. There were too many of them. I found them dizzying. One was that someone carried me in off the street and that someone else had the idea of putting me out in the alley. This someone else either wasn't strong enough to carry me or he didn't care. Either way, he dragged me.

That was the simplest of his reconstructions. Another had it that I had been picked up to be moved into the alley, but realizing that he was being seen by Ethel, the man had carried me inside instead. Then to move me out to the alley he dragged me. That way if Ethel were to talk, he would have made it seem that there had been two people, the one she had seen and another for the second move.

The third was a variant on the second. It was the most ingenious one.

"In moving you around," the inspector said, "the dangerous part of it was at the beginning, those first few feet. That was out in the open. It was then that the guy could be seen. So there at the beginning the big idea was to get under cover, out of sight. The shortest distance to move you out in the open was straight back into the club. It meant getting you into the alley the long way around but the extra distance was a good swap for the reduced exposure."

"Yes, but why the dragging then?"

"Carrying you was tough. Dragging would have been easier, but for those few feet carrying was better. Dragging you, the man would have been fully exposed. Somebody happening to see him would be more likely to recognize him. Bent over under your weight with you hung over his shoulder, he would have been much harder to recognize. It could have been like he was wearing you as a disguise."

"Would anyone actually think of that?" I asked.

"I thought of it," the inspector said.

"But that's you."

"A man who has all his mind fixed on hiding will grab at anything he can use as a cover-up."

"You know," I said. "All those kicks I must have taken, they seem like the most idiotic kind of sadism. I was out cold. I never felt them."

"You're feeling the bruises now."

"Yes, but postponed satisfaction?"

"There could be an explanation there."

"Explanation of what?"

"First you were carried and then you were dragged. You're picked up off the sidewalk and handled gently. He doesn't want to rouse you, at least not until he has you inside where he can do whatever is necessary with you out of the public view. You don't rouse in the carrying, so inside you're dumped on the floor and given the boot. That would have been exploratory, testing the depth of your stupor. It was deep enough. You were in a condition that would do and nobody had to worry about rousing you. You could be dragged out into the alley."

We were not, of course, kicking all this around on the MacPherson doorstep. We had moved to Schmitty's place. I had gone with him in his car and some of it we had done en route. My car I left where I had pulled it up at the MacPherson address. It was only a short walk from there to my apartment. It was in a good enough parking spot. I could walk over later and move it.

CHAPTER 6

Not all these speculations were done without interruption. Schmitty broke it off for a time while he was
hitting the phone. He had himself put through to the
Vice Squad. He was most emphatic with them about
wanting nothing done. All he wanted was information
he expected they would have.

"If it isn't in your records," he said, "one or another
of your guys is likely to know or maybe some quiet and
tactful asking around if that should be necessary."

What he wanted first of all was information on Ethel
Cameron. Where did she live? Was she working alone
or was there someone pimping for her? If the latter,
who? Beyond that he wanted to know whether they
might have anything on a MacPherson at the address
where we had left Ethel. He said this MacPherson
might be a man or a woman.

Finally he read off to them the full list of names he
had taken off the bells at the MacPherson address.
That last struck me as unnecessary. I had seen her hit
the MacPherson bell and I had told him so. I would
have liked it if he could have trusted me that much. I
didn't quite say it, but I suppose I said enough or
showed enough for him to make a good guess at what
was chewing on me.

"She rang the MacPherson bell," he said. "We know
that. You were watching her and you saw it."

"I did. So what's now with all the other people in the house?"

"She was in a hurry to get in. She hadn't wanted us to take her home. Around her own place she didn't want to take any chance on being seen with you or me. So she has you take her to a house where she isn't known. MacPherson can be a friend. MacPherson can be nobody she knows. You're watching her. She rings the MacPherson bell just to get the buzzer release on the vestibule door. That gets her in, but she goes to another apartment. We won't know which."

"Or," I said, "she doesn't know anyone there. She rang any bell at random just so she could put that front door between herself and us. She waited inside in the hall until we had taken off and then came out."

"Possible," Schmitty said, "but unlikely. If she had been doing that, it would have been stupid to pick a bell for a lower floor. You try the top floor and you are less likely to be tangling with an enraged tenant. It takes time for somebody up there to come downstairs. I'm guessing it's a house she knew, a place where she could be sure a doorbell would be answered. Pick a house like that at random and you can run into a nobody-home situation. It's more likely she knew there would be an answer to the MacPherson bell."

"The bell," I said. "What about the bell? How could she believe we'd think she lives there when we saw her ring the bell? Where you live do you ring doorbells? Don't you have a latchkey?"

"Maybe she has a latchkey," the inspector said. "Then she rang the doorbell to give us the idea that it isn't where she lives. She could have wanted us to think she was going visiting. After all, if she lied when she said she crossed the avenue because she had to go

south to go home, was she going to bring out a latchkey and give us a clue to what was sour in her statement? Also she didn't say she was going home. She just
gave you an address. There can be nothing at all to
this address stuff."

It's the inspector's method and I know it. He works
out all the possibilities and he keeps an open mind on
all of them. The simplest and the most likely one he
will explore first. Only when facts emerge that make
him discard this first theory will he turn to another,
but all the while he has been carrying the full range of
them in his head. For him it's an orderly and effective
way of operating. For me it generates nothing but dizzying confusion.

In mental flight from just such confusion my
thoughts tripped over something I had been permit-
ting to slip my mind. It was late to be thinking about
it, but once I had recalled it, it began taking on for me
the shape of an opportunity missed. Initially, I suppose, I would have expected nothing much of it but
then I had been having great expectations of what
Ethel Cameron would be giving us. Now that the
Cameron information seemed to be at least sullied, the
lost opportunity began to look as though it might have
held some greater promise.

"Jocko," I said. "The sonofa who whipped up the
mickey for me."

"Yes," Schmitty said. "Big enough and husky
enough. He could have picked you up and carried you
easily enough, but so could your wrestler buddy or just
about any of those big babes in the chorus line."

"Not that," I said. "He came to visit me. I passed
him up for Ethel. I'm beginning to think I made a mistake."

"What do you mean you passed him up?"

I explained. Although the inspector was interested, he wasn't sharing my distress.

"The way he's been talking," he said, "it'll take one hell of a big turnaround before he'll come up with anything that could do you any good. That baby's no friend of yours."

"You don't think a change of heart?"

I asked the question even though I could find no way of thinking it so myself. I just wanted to hope.

"There's got to be a heart to change," Schmitty said. "And even if there was, there's not much he can change that won't leave him with his own neck stuck out. I can't see him doing that."

"Then why would he have come around?" I asked. "He was there right out front, across the street."

"He could have been watching in the hope of getting something on you to pile on top of all the stuff he's already saying. He may have had ideas about leaning on you some. He can't be happy about what you've been saying about him. He may have come around for nothing more than to hand you a punch in the mouth. The guy is stupid enough for that."

"So we forget him?"

"So we remember him. We even go looking for him."

"He'll hardly be there anymore, not after all this time," I said.

The inspector agreed that it wasn't likely but he wasn't prepared to rule it out.

"He stayed across the street," he said. "He made no move to approach you. So if it was that he wanted to talk to you or to beat up on you, or whatever, he wanted to get you alone. We don't know that he isn't a patient type, biding his time, waiting for you to come home."

We went around to my place to check, but the street was empty of loiterers.

"Okay," the inspector said. "We go to see him."

It was early for The Topless Towers, well before show time, but that didn't mean the bar wouldn't be open. It did mean that business was light. Jocko wasn't behind the bar. His substitute, however, wasn't unknown to me. It was Rich Dawson.

As soon as we were in the door, he spotted me. Whipping out from behind the bar, he headed for me. We weren't even past the hatcheck girl before he was planted in front of me, barring my way.

"Out," he said.

I expected the inspector to have something to say to that, but he hung back. He was even acting as though we weren't together. He wasn't even knowing me. He just walked past my confrontation with Dawson. Bellying up to the bar, he stood there waiting for service. He could have been any customer who'd walked in off the street.

"What do you mean 'out'?" I was standing my ground.

"Out. O-U-T. Out. Get lost. You're not wanted in here, not ever."

"Why?"

"I don't have to tell you any why. You go or I throw you out. That's all."

"Who says? You or The Face?"

"If you got to know, it's The Face. Them are his orders. He don't want you in here."

"He's going to have to tell me that himself."

"He don't have to do nothing. I'm telling and, when I'm through with you, you'll stay told."

"Where's Jocko?" I asked.

"Never no mind where's Jocko. It's Jocko's day off, but from him it'd be the same like from me. He don't want no part of you neither."

"Then why did he come around to my place this afternoon? What was that for? To tell me to stay away from here?"

"I don't know nothing about that."

"But I do," I said.

I'd had no expectation that our exchange could have gone on so long at nothing more than this verbal level. I'd had Dawson pegged as a man of few words, a man of action. Astonishingly he was now all talk and no moves. I was beginning to think that he was only putting on an act. His heart wasn't in it. Nothing could have been more obvious than that Dawson was a man who would put his muscle where his heart was. Although he was still barring my way, he was making not the first move toward laying a hand on me.

Playing the role of the patient customer whose patience was something less than unlimited, Inspector Schmidt broke it up.

"Doesn't anybody tend bar around here?" he said. "How thirsty must a man get?"

He even managed to sound plaintive, and this was the inspector. In all the time I have known him, he has never mixed alcohol with investigation. The last thing he would have been wanting was a drink. He was going to be ordering a beer, but that would be only for establishing a reason for his presence in the club.

I don't think it was wishful thinking that made me

feel Dawson welcomed the interruption. Without another word he walked away from me and went back behind the bar. I took the opportunity to move in and belly up alongside Inspector Schmidt.

"Sorry, mister," Dawson said. "What's your pleasure?"

Schmitty ordered the requisite beer. Dawson drew it and put it on the bar in front of him. Then he temporized with the bartender's standard routine. He swabbed the bar. The silence grew heavier by the moment. It was going to have to break of its own weight. It did.

Dawson turned to me. "Look, mister," he said. "You ain't getting no service here. All you can get yourself here is trouble. What do you want that for?"

"I'd just like to know why everybody all of a sudden is dumping on me," I said. "You and me, last time we were friendly."

"That was last time and anyway I'm being friendly. I don't want to have to throw you out. So now you be friendly and don't make me do it."

"The Face and I, we parted friends."

"Yeah, but he didn't know you was poison. He didn't know you was going to be bad for business. What are you trying to do? Get him closed down?"

"If he's closed down, I won't be the one doing it."

"You won't because you're going to be to hell out of here and quick. You're going to make me throw you out."

He started out from behind the bar. He hadn't taken more than the first step before the inspector spoke up.

"You can't do that," he said.

All the indications were for Dawson to ask who was

going to stop him, but instead he seemed to be all too ready to be stopped. Staying where he was, he addressed himself to the inspector.

"Why?" he asked.

There was nothing of challenge in the way he spoke the word. He sounded as though he were merely asking for enlightenment. Confronted with something he had no wish to do, he was hoping that he would be given some adequate reason for not doing it.

"It's against the law," Schmitty said.

"What law? The Face, he owns this club. He don't want somebody here, it's his property. He don't have to have anybody in it he don't want."

"'A man's home is his castle,' but this is no home." In no way was Inspector Schmidt throwing his weight around. He was just playing the part of the barroom philosopher. "This is a place of public accommodation. Nobody can be barred from a place of public accommodation. It's the Fourteenth Amendment."

"Guys they get thrown out of saloons all the time. I've thrown them out in my time plenty myself. Nobody's ever had no law on me."

"If a man's creating a disturbance or if a man's drinking and won't pay, yes, sure. But this gentleman is quiet. He's behaving himself. You have no legitimate reason for refusing him service. So you can't do it. You see, if he needs a witness, I'll speak for him."

In Dawson's ears the last of that must have carried some small sound of threat. The Rich Dawsons of this world know of only one way of responding to threat. They take up the challenge. They go hostile.

"Looks like I'm going to have to throw the both of you out, him and you," Dawson said, and now his move out from behind the bar was taking on a new purposefulness.

"That," the inspector said, "will be an even worse mistake."

That didn't stop Dawson. He kept advancing on us.

"Yeah? And who's going to be your witness? Him?"

"As dumb moves go," Schmitty said, "assaulting a police officer is the all-time beaut."

"Who's a cop?"

The inspector brought out his credentials. Dawson read them. He was a long time reading them. He may have been working on every last word of the fine print, but I think not. It was more likely that reading was one of Rich Dawson's less developed skills. Eventually he handed them back. He also backed off, returning to his place behind the bar.

"You just come in for the beer?" he asked. "Or you want something else?"

"Since I'm here," Schmitty said, "I too would like to hear the answer to the gentleman's question. Why are you dumping on him?"

"It's orders. I only work here."

"The bar or one of the girls?"

"I got a girl. Law against that?"

"The dead man, Paul Peters, he'd done a number on her."

"That was before I knowed her. If I had been around back then, he wouldn't have lived so long."

"And now he's dead."

"The black tie, it ain't for him." Dawson was indicating his traditional bartender's bow.

"I asked you if you worked the bar or one of the girls," the inspector said.

"I just told you. I got a girl."

"Just for yourself or are you running her?"

"What kind of a question is that?"

"Call it a cop's question."

"You make it real hard not hitting a cop," Dawson said.

"I suppose that means you're telling me she's just for yourself."

"That's right. I'm telling you."

"So now we can go back to the first question," Schmitty said.

"What's that?"

"This gentleman, here."

Dawson scowled. "It's no accident you two came in here together," he said. "You're this friend he's got him on the cops. I know all about you. You'll be putting in the fix for him. We was warned about that. You'll do it by framing somebody else."

"Who told you that?"

"The news gets around."

"Is Drew having the day off?" the inspector asked.

"Who's he?"

"The Face."

"He's around. Out back, upstairs. He's around."

"Go tell him we want to talk to him."

"He gave me my orders. I wasn't to leave this guy in the place."

"Drew? He's only a little guy. You scared of him?"

"He owns the club. He gives the orders. It gets run the way he wants it run."

"You tell him that with Inspector Schmidt around you can't run it the way he wants it."

There was an intercom deal behind the bar. Dawson

pushed some buttons and shouted into it. We could hear The Face come on.

"I hear you, Rich," he said. "Even without the wires I'd hear you. So what's your problem?"

"Him. He's here and I couldn't keep him out because of he's got his cop buddy, that there Inspector Schmidt, along with him."

"It's okay," The Face said. "For this once it's okay. He won't be murdering anybody while he's under police surveillance, even if it's friendly surveillance."

"The cop, he wants to see you."

"He saw me before. Since when am I so good to look at?"

Inspector Schmidt had the bar between him and the intercom. He tried shouting.

"You're beautiful," he said. "Either way you like it. You come out here or we go around back to look for you."

"No good right now," The Face said. "I'm in conference."

"Like he's General Motors," Schmitty said, turning to me. "Let's go. We can confer as well as the next man."

Since I'd been that route, I was prepared to show Schmitty the way back to the dressing rooms, but he took the lead. I should have expected as much. It was obvious that he would be carrying around in his head a detailed floor plan of the scene of the crime.

Short of the dressing-room doors there was a flight of stairs. The inspector went only that far. At the foot of the stairs he stopped for a moment to listen. I listened with him. There was someone on the stairs, running down them. He wasn't on that bottom flight. We couldn't see him. We could only hear him somewhere up above. The inspector started up and I was following after him. We were going to meet The Face or his conferee halfway.

There was nothing stealthy about the way the inspector was moving. He was taking the steps two at a time in a pounding run. Almost immediately we could hear the steps above us do a reverse. The man who had been running down was now racing back up. The footsteps stopped and a door clanged. The inspector also did a quick reverse. Taking me by surprise, he all but knocked me over as he raced past me. I wasn't as quick, but, nevertheless, I made it in time.

I wouldn't have known the way, but keeping close to the inspector's heels, I couldn't go wrong. He had told me earlier that there was an elevator. The door to the shaft was down a hall past the dressing-room doors and just inside the back exit that gave access to the alley. Since in my one disastrous visit to the dump, The Face had decided against my leaving by the alley, I hadn't seen that part of the backstage area.

It was there that the inspector headed. I had been at a loss to understand what was going on, but once I was standing with Inspector Schmidt at the door to the elevator shaft, everything became clear. There had been the clanging door. Doors to rooms don't clang. They might creak. An unoiled hinge might squeal. They might bang, but clang they do not.

Someone had been racing down the stairs on his way out of the place. This someone had been intent on avoiding a confrontation with Inspector Schmidt. Cut off on the stairs, he had doubled back and was coming down in the elevator. His calculation had to be that he would be out of the elevator, through the alley door, and gone before we could have been off the stairs.

We could hear the hum of the descending car. It was oozing slowly down the shaft emitting a sound that was like a prolonged sigh. We heard it click to a stop. The shaft door opened. There was only one man in the car. He had been moving forward. At the sight of us, however, he took a backward step instead.

He was in retreat, but it was a move foredoomed to futility. Another step would have brought him up against the back wall of the car. He made a try at looking like a man who had forgotten something and was waiting for the elevator door to close so that he could ride back upstairs. Taking hold of the door, the inspector held it open.

"Are you getting out," he asked, "or will we be riding up together?"

The man didn't answer. Instead he just moved to leave the car. The inspector moved with him, planting himself with his back to the alley door. It was only then that the man spoke.

"Excuse me," he said.

"What for?" Schmitty said. "Have you done something?"

"Very funny. You're barring my way."

"Probably not for long. We will just talk a little and then we'll see."

The man shrugged. "So talk, but make it fast. I haven't much time."

"Who are you?"

"Nobody."

"That's too modest. Everybody is somebody."

"I thought it would be more polite than telling you it was none of your business."

I knew this guy and I was working hard at trying to place him. He had the kind of looks that should have made him difficult if not impossible to forget. His face was all bristling beard and horn-rimmed spectacles. You could call it the face of a professor. It was the way they looked about a century ago. In university photographs of old-time faculties you'll see them. For a long time then professors seemed to be of another breed, but now there has been this new lot, young savants who, giving up on the razor, are cultivating the hairy, old-time look.

On the face alone I would probably have had no memory of him, but the man had a body that was so much at odds with his head that you could have thought he was wearing some other guy's face. From the chin down he could easily have been one of the challengers who met Rich Dawson on the mat.

It was not only that he was big and that he had the burliest kind of muscularity. He also had the hands of a ditchdigger. His fingernails were black-rimmed. Dirt had been so much ground in that it had become inseparable from the leathery skin of his hands.

It was this curious combination of bookish face and laborer's hands that made the guy's appearance memorable. He was nobody I knew well, but I was certain that he was someone I had at one time or another met or possibly even at one time or another just seen. It was at that sort of level that I was finding him familiar.

He showed, furthermore, a similar dichotomy in his way of speaking. His speech was at once cultivated and tough. The faultless enunciation and impeccable grammar belonged to the face. The toughness of the tone belonged to the hands and the body.

"If we are going to be polite," Schmitty said, "let

me break the ice and introduce myself." He made it complete. "Inspector Schmidt, Chief of Homicide, N.Y.P.D."

"I'm impressed, Inspector," the man said, "but your business isn't with me. You are keeping me from an appointment."

It was during this exchange that my memory slipped into gear. Once it had made the connection, it seemed so obvious that I was annoyed at its not having done it sooner.

"We've met," I said.

"Have we? You'll forgive me. I have no recollection of it."

There was no reason why he should have remembered. It had been an introduction at a large party a year or more back. It had been brief, casual, and without any follow-up. Since it had been a party of sleek and suave characters, just on appearance and manner he had been a standout. The introduction had come about only because, wondering about him, I had asked who he was and what he did.

He operated somewhere on the outer rim of the world of artists and art galleries. He collected and dealt in architectural ornaments salvaged from demolished buildings. I had been thinking of gangland types and of nightclub business and liquor salesmen. If I had kept in mind The Face's hobby—and surely there had been every reason why I should have had that very much in mind—I wouldn't have been so long in remembering.

"You're André Bartholomew," I said. "You're the big man in the kind of thing The Face has been collecting."

"Am I?"

"I've seen some of the collection he has here," I said. "He must be just about your best customer."

I was trying to make it sound like idle conversation though I don't understand why I should have thought it necessary. I was doing it, of course, for the inspector's information.

He picked it up. "See, Mr. Bartholomew," he said. "You never know. I do have business with you."

Bartholomew chose to misinterpret that. "Buying or selling?" he said. "If you are buying, what are you in the market for? If you are selling, what have you got?"

"I'm investigating a murder and, since you are a dealer in lethal weapons . . ."

"Hardly that, Inspector Schmidt."

"You sold the stone dragon."

"No. I didn't."

"You didn't sell it? The Face didn't buy it from you?"

"That's right."

"Called as a witness, you'd testify under oath that you didn't sell it to him?"

"No problem there."

"You mean you're ready to swear to it."

"Anytime."

"Does that mean it's a fact or that you are careless about perjury?"

"If you can ask the question," Bartholomew said, "what would make you believe my answer?"

"That might depend on what you answered," Schmitty said.

Bartholomew laughed. "Yes," he said. "If I told you I was careless about perjury, you would believe me," he said.

Schmitty laughed with him. "How could I," he said, "if you were that honest about it?"

"I didn't sell him the dragon," Bartholomew said, "and he didn't buy it."

I was wondering at this going on for so long with The Face staying out of it. I was quite certain that he was lurking around some corner of that little hall and listening. It seemed likely that he was well pleased with the way the questions and answers were going and was seeing no reason for trying to break it up.

"He didn't buy it from you," Schmitty said. "It's your kind of thing and there can't be so many people in the trade that you wouldn't know all of them and know what they are doing. Who did he buy it from?"

"He didn't buy it."

"You can't be sure of that. Who had it in stock?"

"I am sure. I can be sure because I had it in stock."

"And you sold it. Who bought it from you?"

"Nobody. It was one of the best things I ever handled and I was asking a suitable price for it. It turned out to be too steep for my regular customers. I was ready to hold it and wait for my price."

"But you didn't wait."

"It was taken out of my hands. It was stolen."

"Burglary?"

"Yes."

"You didn't report it to the police."

"An exercise in futility, Inspector. Have the police ever been known to recover anyone's stolen property?"

CHAPTER 7

He didn't know who stole it. He didn't know how it got to the roof that topped The Topless Towers. He had no ideas. He made no attempt to conceal the fact that he was happiest with not knowing and not having any ideas.

About the time that the inspector had had from Bartholomew just about everything he could have hoped to have, The Face came trotting down the stairs. He put on a look of astonishment so intense that you could have bottled it and sold it as a concentrate to be diluted with three containers of water. The man, after all, was an actor, but he was misjudging his effect. Projected across the footlights, it might have worked. At closer range it was too much. It was directed at Bartholomew.

"You still here?" he said. "You had an appointment. You were in a hurry."

"I was detained," Bartholomew said.

"Sorry." Leaving it at just the one word, The Face turned from Bartholomew to speak to the inspector. "There's no reason for you to be holding this man," he said. "Anything you want to know from him, you can ask me. He doesn't know anything I don't know. We've been over the whole thing together."

"Agreeing on your story?" Schmitty asked.

"No story," The Face said. "Any story I had a part in would be funny. Don't forget I'm a comic."

"The story I've just been handed is funny."

"Semantics, Inspector," The Face said. "You're talking about funny-peculiar. I make with the funny-haha. So, since nobody's laughing . . ."

Engaged now with The Face, the inspector moved away from the alley door. Bartholomew edged past him and took hold of the doorknob. His movements were tentative. It seemed to me that he was trying to make them furtive. He would have liked to slip away unnoticed, but the four of us were too much at close quarters for anything like that. The inspector turned back to him.

"When I need you," he said, "where will I find you?"

Bartholomew brought a business card out of his pocket and pushed it at the inspector.

"Mostly I'm not there," he said.

"It'll be handier if I can look for you where you will be. Where mostly you won't be can't be expected to do anyone much good."

"I can be anywhere," Bartholomew explained. "All the time, all over the city, buildings are coming down. Anyplace there's a wrecking crew, that's where I have to be. My answering service takes messages. Anytime you give me a call, I'll call you back."

"I'll expect that," Schmitty said.

"You can count on it and now I've got to run."

"Okay," the inspector said. "I'll be calling you."

"Anything I can do to help."

With that Bartholomew took off. The Face waited until the door had shut behind him. When he spoke, it was in the manner of a man who is talking to himself.

It was obvious, however, that he wanted to be over-heard.

"Funny-peculiar," he said. "A man who can't lie any better than that ought to realize that he's stuck with the truth. It's no good his trying."

"You know his story?"

"He rehearsed it on me. How often does it happen, Inspector? You trace something to its owner and he tells you it was stolen and he didn't bother to report it."

"That's murder cars," I said.

"Just cars? Not ever murder weapons?"

"What was he doing here?" the inspector asked.

"Nothing. Not a damn thing. I called him and asked him to come. I might as well have not bothered."

"What did you want of him?"

"Only that he make me a decent offer. I've got some great stuff. Stuff like I've got he's never going to see again."

"Let's move this someplace where we can sit down," Schmitty said.

"Upstairs."

The Face waved us toward the elevator. He was making his choice of where we would be going to sit and talk. We were only a few steps away from his dressing room and we could have been comfortable in there. Even upstairs he led us past rooms that looked more comfortable than the one he chose. It was a room that didn't even have three chairs in it. He had to drag one in from another room.

The place where he settled us looked like nothing but a storeroom. It contained what had to be the least interesting part of his collection. In it there were run-of-the-mill cornice blocks, column caps, column bases,

and drums that might be fitted together to make col-
umns. There wasn't a thing in there that wasn't represented at least in duplicate. For some items I could see
as many as four or five identical pieces.

The inspector looked the room over. "You called him
in and asked him to make you an offer on this crap you
have in here?" he asked.

"The whole thing," The Face said. "This crap, the
good stuff, the great stuff, every last hunk of it. I want
to unload and start a new collection. This time it's
going to be objects smaller than a man's hand and
nothing that has a point on it. Buttons for instance.
Can anyone kill with buttons?"

"Bullets," Schmitty said.

"They're pointed."

"They can also be blunt-nosed. Those are specially
nasty."

The Face sighed. "Yeah," he said, "and one of those
little derringers. Maybe it will have to be soft things
smaller than a man's hand. This is going to take re-
thinking. Maybe butterflies."

"And this junk," the inspector said. "You're not
thinking you'll have any use for it ever again?"

"Use for it?" The Face made a sweeping gesture that
encompassed the total contents of the room. "What do
you know about collectors, Inspector?"

"I listen to what the shrinks tell me," Schmitty said,
"but that's dirty talk. Some collectors do it for invest-
ment. Keep junk long enough and it becomes valuable
only because nobody else thought to hang on to it.
Some do it out of an uncontrollable lust for owning
things. Then there are some that are just crazies."

"Collectors like to have things complete," The Face
said. "They want the rare items. They most specially

want unique items, something nobody else has or can have. They want the rarities. They want the interesting examples. They want all that, but they also want the nothing items. It's not that those mean anything. It's just that without them the collection isn't complete."

"So?"

"So, take a look at what I got here. There isn't an item I haven't got twice, three times, even more times over. If I was looking for something I could tip over the roof parapet, I could have taken anything out of this room and the collection wouldn't be any the less complete. Take any one of these things. It's plenty heavy enough to do what the dragon's tail did. So can anybody imagine that I, a collector, would choose to do important damage to my collection by smashing the dragon's tail? It leaves an important and unique item incomplete."

"I can," Schmitty said.

"Tell me how you can."

"It was up on the roof ready to hand and it wasn't part of your collection. You didn't own it. That's what you say anyhow."

"I didn't own it, but I wanted to own it someday. I wouldn't fix things so I could never own it. Up on the roof? Okay. Let's go up there."

He led the way. Up there he paused for a moment of silent mourning before the St. George figure and the dragon amputee. Breaking out of his lugubrious reverie, he urged the inspector to examine the ravaged group and to compare it with the other pieces displayed in that rooftop setting. He made the point that it was the only thing up there that could ever draw so much as a second look. Every other item on the roof was yet another copy of what he had in multiple copies down in that room from which we had just come.

"Up here is no place to keep anything you care about preserving," he said. "Acid rain, abrasive grit, air pollution. Stone, concrete, name it—it just gets eaten up. Up here I keep the junk, never a St. George and the dragon the like of which nobody's ever going to see again. Things like that I keep downstairs where I can enjoy them and where they're in no danger of damage."

"But the thing was up here."

"Only because I didn't know it was. I didn't own it. Someone put it up here without my knowing. I often go months without ever coming up here."

"I find that hard to believe," the inspector said.

"As soon as you get someplace where you can check out the soot on your collar," The Face said, "you'll believe. Stay up here long enough and you come down ready to sing 'Mammy' without needing to cork up."

He was going to need a better diversion than that if he was to have any hope of diverting Inspector Schmidt.

"I find it hard to believe that this could have been stolen from Bartholomew and brought up here to your roof without your knowing it," Schmitty said. "If it wasn't stolen by you or by someone acting as your agent, how would it have gotten up here? That's a big hunk of stuff for anyone to have sneaked into the building and brought up here without your knowledge. That's what I find hard to believe."

"And why wouldn't you?" The Face said. "It isn't easy for me either. The stuff that's easy to believe is the stuff guys make up. When a guy embroiders himself a lie, he sews credibility into the design. The truth doesn't need to be believable. It just is."

"It can't be impossible," the inspector said.

"What's impossible? A delivery is trucked up to the alley door. It's hauled inside and loaded on the elevator. By elevator it goes up here to the roof where it is unloaded and set down handy to the edge where you can look down into the alley. All that's more than possible. It's easy."

"Without your knowing anything about it? Without your knowing it was hauled in and brought up here?"

The Face argued that it was far easier to believe that it had been done without his knowledge than to think for a moment that he could have known it was up on the roof exposed to all the destructive elements and that he would have left it up there. He was acting as though it had already been established and accepted by all parties concerned that he could never have been guilty of maiming such a rarity as St. George's dragon. He was now working within a much narrower compass.

At show time, he said, the alley door was rarely locked. Even during cold nights and for winter it had been a warm night—hadn't I lain sweating first out on the sidewalk and later in the alley without catching my death of pneumonia?—the girls and even The Face himself always came offstage needing to cool down.

"We go out to the alley and grab a smoke," he said. "All of us going in and out that way, we're not locking any of us out, and even the last one in, who remembers to lock the door?"

So there had been all those periods when he and the Towers had been onstage. A delivery made then could easily have been accomplished without anyone's knowledge.

"Maybe it was that same night," he said, "or the night before or even before that. I don't remember when I was last up here on the roof. It's been two weeks—at the least two weeks."

"Which night doesn't matter," the inspector said, "if it could have been any night."

"André says the same night," The Face said. "He says he saw it during the day and then the next morning it was gone."

"And you don't believe him?"

"Do you?"

"I don't believe anybody. It's the way I work."

"He doesn't act like a man who's telling the truth," The Face said. "A valuable piece is stolen from him and he doesn't report it to the police. Sure, you cops aren't hell on wheels when it comes to recovering stolen property for people, but something valuable is stolen, you report it just on the chance. Even the cops can sometimes pass a miracle. What did he have to lose? Also doesn't he carry insurance? What chance has he with the insurance company on an unreported theft?"

"You think like a detective," Schmitty said.

"Have you ever noticed, Inspector? You have a man with his ass in a vise, there's nothing like it for making a man think."

"And when a man is sore at a guy who wouldn't make him a good offer, it can set the direction for his thinking."

"One direction or another, Inspector," The Face said, "thinking is thinking. Here's something else to think about. Why is André Bartholomew scared of the police? Why did he try to get out of here without your seeing him?"

"If he was here so the two of you could get your stories matched up and make sure there would be no contradictions, he could have preferred that I didn't know you'd had a chance to get your heads together."

"Wouldn't that have been more skin off my ass than off his?" The Face asked.

"You say he didn't want me seeing him here? What's to say it wasn't you who didn't want that? You may have been the one who was trying to get him out without his running into me."

"I had plenty of time for that from when Rich told me you were down at the bar," The Face said. "If I'd told André then, he'd have been out and away before you ever came backstage. I didn't tell him till it was a good time for you to be catching up with him when he was on the run. I wanted to see if he'd run and I didn't want him making it. Call it delicacy, Inspector. I wanted you catching up with him and I didn't want to have to be the one to tell you stuff that would put you on to him. I thought I timed it neatly."

"You don't do everything that neatly," the inspector said.

"What about all the rest of the evidence I've been giving you?" The Face said. "Since I've shown you that I'm telling the truth, I have nothing to be afraid of."

"Okay. You have nothing to be afraid of. For a guy with nothing to fear, why have you been working so hard at trying to frame Bagby?"

"Me? I'm not trying to frame anybody."

"Orders out front that he isn't to be served. Orders that anytime he shows he's to be bounced out quick."

"It's all over the media that he's a murder suspect. He comes into a club and he gets himself falling-down drunk. He gets into a hassle with another customer. He's so drunk, he doesn't know what he's doing. He kills this other customer. It could be it was an accident. Somehow he wandered up to the roof. There's never any telling where a drunk will get to."

"You know none of that's true." I couldn't just listen to him without some protest. The Face rode right over my protest.

"A drunk up there on the roof sees a dragon," he said. "He's too drunk to see it for what it is. He thinks it's for real—maybe not for really real, just for DT's real. He grabs it. He's fighting it. Since it's in sections, the tail comes away in his hands. He heaves that off the roof. It could be like that, an accident. A guy thinks he's handling a dragon, where is he going to take hold of it?" The Face was obviously warming to this fantasy. He was getting carried away with it. "He grabs the dragon," he said, "where he thinks it'll be safe, by the tail. Like with a lobster. You take hold of it just behind the claws where it can't get at you."

While he was spilling all this garbage at us, The Face should at least have blushed. He didn't.

"You're forgetting," Schmitty said, "that in preparation for getting drunk and scaring himself silly with a dragon he first had to steal the dragon and sneak it up to your roof."

The Face sighed. "I've been trying to give him the benefit of the doubt," he said. "But you're right. It can't have been an accident. No way. So you must see how it is. People think he came in here. He got stoned. He murdered another customer. After all that I still let him hang out here? Is that good for business? Have a heart, Inspector. That way lies bankruptcy."

"You know better than that," Schmitty said. "You just don't know a drawing card when one comes your way."

"All right. I didn't think I'd have to tell you and I didn't want to say it. You talk about what you can't believe. So I can't believe you don't know that the word's out on him."

"What word?"

"The DA's office word, the City Hall word, the Albany word. For all I know, maybe even the White House word. Paul Peters was only P.P. to me but he pulled a lot of weight in other places. The people in those other places, I can't let them think there's anything but a lot of space between me and Bagby. I want to stay in business and I want to stay alive."

"Dead men pull no weight. Peters is dead."

"Dead or alive, P.P. pulls weight. There are too many people who don't want any hint getting out that there could have been any reason for his getting knocked off. If he was that kind of a bastard, people will be asking how come all those babies who are the darlings of the Moral Majority let themselves be so close to him. The way they want it is a pointless murder done by an irresponsible drunk. Without our friend here, they're fresh out of an irresponsible drunk."

He had the grace to say he was sorry and to add in strict confidence just among the three of us that in his own heart he knew I was an all-right guy, but he quickly followed it by telling me that I wasn't without fault in the matter.

"You should never have had that last drink," he said.

"The only reason you were going out past the bar was so you wouldn't tangle with P.P. You didn't have to stop for another drink. That was your idea. Without that last drink you would have been okay."

"And whose idea was it to make it a mickey?" I asked.

"It wasn't a mickey."

"Who says?"

"Jocko and he ought to know. He poured it for you."

"And his mickeys are much admired," I said. "Those are your own words. You also said they come full strength."

"True and true," The Face said. "So with every reason the man is proud of his mickeys. He wouldn't make one and then disown it. If that had been a mickey he made you, he would be boasting about it."

"I thought you saved all the jokes for the stage," I said.

"He poured it right in front of you, he says. You were watching him all the time."

We were getting nowhere. Inspector Schmidt stepped back into it.

"He came around to see Bagby this afternoon," Schmitty said.

The Face was taken by surprise. He temporized.

"Who?" he asked.

"Jocko."

"He did? What did he want?"

"He didn't get to talk to Bagby. Bagby was otherwise engaged."

"Do you think he came around to boast about his mickey?" I asked.

The Face laughed. "I wouldn't put it past him," he said. "But you did watch him pour it, didn't you?"

"I did, but that doesn't say the contents of the bottle matched the label."

"No, no," The Face said. "They have to match. You can't refill bottles. There's a law against it."

I hadn't thought Inspector Schmidt would possibly have been content to leave it at that. I had a head full of questions and I'd been expecting he would have been asking them. It seemed to me that they were crying to be asked. I couldn't believe that they hadn't occurred to the inspector. We pulled out of The Topless Towers. As soon as we'd hit the street, I brought them up.

"What about all the other questions?" I asked.

"What other questions?"

"Who carried me in off the street? Who dragged me out to the alley?"

"And who went up to the roof and dropped the dragon's tail on Peters?" Schmitty added.

"All right," I said. "It'd be no good asking him that, but what about the other questions?"

"All in the same basket," the inspector said. "In my first session with him he handed me an alibi to cover all of the critical time. It's not the world's best alibi, but he's put it in the record and he's not going to be backing away from it."

"When you talked to him before, what was he calling Peters?"

"The same as just now. He likes the initials."

"Talking to me, he called Peters The Golden Creep."

"Hardly an unfair estimate of the man," the inspector said.

"That's the way he felt about the guy. Peters is murdered in his alley. Peters is murdered with a hunk of sculpture tossed off his roof. He says it wasn't his.

Bartholomew admits to owning it, but says it was stolen from him. All that adds up to Drew needing an alibi, doesn't it?"

"So he has one or he was smart enough to cook himself up a phony. Unless I can crack it, he has himself covered for all the time that counts."

After sending me off to go out the front way, he had, according to the story he had given the inspector, done a quick job of removing his make-up. Since he never wore much, he explained that removing it was no lengthy process. Changing out of costume had also been quick and easy. It involved no more than a change of pants—out of the baggy ones into a pair with a crease.

"As soon as he was changed," the inspector told me, "he says he took off. He went out through the alley. On all the stories we've collected we have only Drew saying he went that way. Your bartender friend, Jocko, says he went out the front way since that's the way he always goes. It's only the people who leave from backstage who ever go out through the alley."

"That," I said, "seems reasonable enough for any ordinary night, but it wasn't an ordinary night."

"For them it was an ordinary night. Nobody is going to admit anything else. What wasn't ordinary happened without their knowing anything about it and after they had all left. They saw you lying on the sidewalk out front and they just left you. They thought you were in a drunken sleep."

"They thought?"

"They say that's what it looked like and they have no way of knowing that you couldn't have roused and gone into action."

"They want to leave that possibility open," I said.

According to the story The Face had given Inspector Schmidt, when he had gone through the alley, there had been nobody by the alley door or anywhere else the length of the alley but Peters. At that time, The Face swore, Peters had been alone and undamaged, completely his usual self, waiting for the girls to come out.

Since he had been there and waiting, however, the Towers were to leave by the street door. Those had been the instructions from the boss and Rich Dawson had been there to see that the instructions were followed.

"All the stories match," Schmitty said. "The dames and Dawson all swear they went out by the street door and nobody saw Peters in the alley, mashed or unmashed, alive or dead."

"Okay. The Face said he changed and went out. Is that all the alibi he gave you?"

"Drew? Drew's a brain. He has a good alibi, complete with confirmation."

"But breakable?"

"When you have alibi witnesses and all of them are your man's good friends, it doesn't necessarily mean that the alibi's a phony. People very often do spend time in the company of their friends. It does mean though that, if it should be a phony, breaking it is going to depend on how friendship might balance off against pressure."

The inspector ran off for me the names of the alibi witnesses. If there was a top jazzman who wasn't on the list, it could only have been that he was off on the road and therefore not available for that after-hours session at which the musicians, having finished their night's work in the various clubs around town, came together to jam what was left of the night away.

"All those guys swear he was with them?"

"Not a blueblower around who doesn't."

"That isn't likely," I said. "He isn't a musician. He's a comic. What was he doing at a jam session?"

"He's their Number One fan, they say, and they also say he's a very funny man. They like to keep him around for laughs."

Peters, you must recognize, hadn't come to anything like a quiet end. The dragon's tail had not only crashed down on his head. It had shattered on the pavement of the alley. The noise of that must have been terrific. So there was nobody who was admitting to having been within earshot of it.

"You've got at least one liar," I said, "if not two."

"The killer perhaps," Schmitty said.

"What makes it perhaps?" I asked. "Somebody killed Peters and since everybody's saying he wasn't around at the time . . ."

"Everybody but you and maybe Ethel Cameron."

"You know what I mean."

"I know that you're thinking it has to be somebody who was in the club and who is lying about having left while Peters was still unmashed. That's not necessarily so."

He explained it to me. According to the story he'd had from The Face, the door to the alley had been locked. Even though The Face was to have been the last one to use that door, he hadn't wanted Peters to see him lock it. The girls always took longer changing out of costume. They couldn't be as quick about it as The Face. They had still been in their dressing room when Drew had taken off and he was doing nothing to tip Peters to the fact that, when they left, they would not be coming through the alley.

"Did he say it was locked or not locked?" I asked.

"He says he left it unlocked, but that Jocko locked it from the inside. That's his story and it's Jocko's. Drew says that when he came home from the jam session, he went in the front way and, before he went upstairs, he checked the alley door to make sure it was locked. He says he checked it from the inside and it was locked."

"So, according to all of them, it would have to be that Peters just went on waiting in the alley until after they had all gone off. I don't believe that. He was out in the alley and he had his goon in the club. Everybody paraded out the front way and Peters never got the word? The man was knocked off before they were all out of there. Nothing else is possible."

"That will make it a lot more than your two liars," Schmitty said. "It will be Jocko, Dawson, and all the girls."

"And that wouldn't surprise me at all."

"Everybody in on it?"

"Everybody in a concerted effort to frame me."

"Come on! You can't be that unpopular."

"I'm that convenient. There's his man, Henry. Can he be expected to hold still for his boss being murdered? Won't he be going after somebody? If they're all scared of him, why won't they be trying to put it on someone who takes it away from them? So I'm that someone."

"Fair enough. We're going to have to find Hank and have a talk with him."

"You think he knows and he's planning to handle it himself?"

"Could be. It can also be that he doesn't know but that they've sold him on you and he's just waiting for his chance to get at you."

"That's a cheerful thought."

"In this business you can't keep all your thoughts cheerful. You have to face facts, but let's get back to your two liars. Who were you figuring?"

"Whoever it was carried me inside and whoever it was dragged me out to the alley unless they were one and the same. Ethel puts both moves after Peters was dead."

"If we can believe Ethel," Schmitty said.

"Maybe not all of what she told us, but why not that much of it? Why would she lie about that? And it makes sense. I did have to get from the street to the alley."

"You could have been dragged directly into the alley. There's only her story to say you were taken inside."

"Why should she lie about that? It was the one part of her story she didn't want to tell."

"Or it was something she so much wanted to get in that she put on her act of not wanting to tell it, just to make sure it would be the part of her story nobody would think to question. The way she went about telling it you can take it either way."

"But why?"

"It destroys at least one story. If she's telling the truth, then there was at least one person who hadn't left before Peters was killed."

"But that was self-evident from the first," I said. "Somebody was inside to go up to the roof and drop that damn dragon's tail on Peters."

"Not necessarily. The roof can be reached easily

from the roof of the house next door. Over there they have a lock on the downstairs door, but it isn't worth a damn. Anybody can open it. So the killer could have come and gone that way. Maybe she's aware of that and she wants me ruling it out."

"Why?"

"The simplest answer might be that she did it herself."

"Ethel?"

It struck me as the wildest of wild guesses but that was only until the inspector began exploring it for me. Any woman who had been with The Golden Creep, even though she might have put a high value on the material rewards, would almost certainly, despite her enjoyment of those rewards, be left with a wish to kill the man. Everything indicated that Peters had had something of a fix on the Towers but Ethel could be considered to be something in the nature of an appendage to the club.

"A guy's spent an evening in there," Schmitty said, "and it's been all look and no touch. He's overstimulated and he comes out. There's Ethel patrolling outside and just when he's most susceptible. Why couldn't it have been that way with Peters and why couldn't Ethel have come away from it with a determination that one day she was going to get him?"

"And all her solicitude for me," I said, "trying to get me a cab, all that was nothing more than trying to get a possible witness out of the way?"

The inspector had broached it, but he wasn't buying it. "It's nice," he said, "but it's very, very iffy and it leaves too much unexplained. There's all this business about the dragon and how it got up there on the roof."

"Through the house next door," I said. "You were just telling me it's easy."

"The lock's easy, but that's all. There's no elevator next door. It's a walk-up. All that weight wrestled up five floors? The babe isn't that husky. For that matter, I don't think anyone is."

"So we're back to she saw what she says she saw?"

That's the way I operate. I shuttle between yes and no.

Inspector Schmidt finds the way stations of all sorts of maybes. It could have been someone else who had gone through the house next door, someone Ethel would be trying to protect if she wasn't holding him in reserve for purposes of blackmail.

Even if she had been telling the truth, we were still left with more than one reasonable interpretation there. If she had told it unwillingly, then she would be trying to protect one of the club's insiders. If she had been playacting in an effort to make her story convincing, that didn't have to mean that she had been working at putting over a lie.

"That's her regular beat," Schmitty said, "back and forth in front of that Topless Towers dump. Have they been letting her work it just on her own? Does she have a pimp strong enough to lean on them and make them hold still for it? Or is Drew or someone else in the club running her, an extra service available to the club's patrons? Take it that way, and it can go in either direction. There's the girl who loves the procurer and the girl who hates him."

CHAPTER 8

All the time we had been kicking all these possibilities around we had been on a hunt for Jocko. The inspector had his home address, but Jocko wasn't there and the neighbors said he hadn't been home all night. They also said that it was in no way unusual for him to be out all night. The consensus was that he had a woman somewhere and that fairly frequently, when he finished work, he would stay the night with her. That he hadn't been home through most of the day seemed to them more the occasion for comment.

The neighbors knew his schedule. They knew that it was his day off and they were conversant with the pattern of his days off. Invariably he began his off time by having a big night and then the daytime hours would be spent at home asleep. They had seen the newspapers and they had watched TV.

From those sources they were aware that, big night or no, he had been home in the early morning, awake, and under police questioning. The neighbors, however, hadn't seen him then. It had been before their waking time and he hadn't been home since. For that reason it had been generally assumed that there had been more than they had been seeing on TV.

There were those who had been saying he was under arrest. Others had it that he had been detained as an important witness. Now that a police officer had come looking for him, the neighbors didn't know what to think.

Beyond the general certainty that he had one, nobody knew anything about his woman. So nobody had any knowledge of where she lived. At this stage of things there was nothing to warrant putting out any sort of an alarm on him. The following day would have him due back at his post behind the bar at The Topless Towers. There was no reason to think he wouldn't be there.

Giving up on Jocko for the time being, Schmitty headed east toward the river. We came into one of those pockets you'll find around town. New York likes to pretend they're not there. The crumbling tenements have their doors boarded up and window glass has been replaced by metal sheathing.

Those tenements are a chilling sight. They look as though by some act of savagery they had been blinded. One likes to think that all life has gone out of them, but derelicts and bag ladies find a way of sifting back into them despite all efforts to dislodge them.

Interspersed with the tenements and in only a slightly better state of repair are big, faceless, red-brick structures. They once were breweries or busy warehouses. Now, if they are not abandoned, they house enterprises that teeter along the narrow rim of bankruptcy.

You could hardly conceive of a less likely area in which to do business, but in these areas business is done. Outfits that cannot survive if they are to pay more than a minimal rent now tenant these warehouses that in earlier times were rich and fat.

Inspector Schmidt pulled up in front of one of them. It was the address he had for André Bartholomew's place of business. As these buildings go, it was one of the smaller ones. It looked dilapidated but that was only because its brickwork was heavily begrimed and its massive metal doors and the iron bars at its windows were badly in need of paint. The door was securely locked and no light showed through the windows. There was a bell, but there was no response to the inspector's ring.

There was no reason to have expected one. Bartholomew had told us that he was seldom there, and we had come to it at an hour when few places of business would have been open. It was now well into the evening. Schmitty evinced no disappointment. He busied himself in an examination of the door and its lock. I couldn't see that they required any such close inspection.

"The place is a fortress," I said. "How could a burglar ever get in?"

"By blasting the lock, and since this isn't any new lock, you can rule that out."

"Could it be picked?" I asked.

"There's no lock that can't be handled," Schmitty said, "if a man knows how and he has the right tools and enough time. He would also want to be working without an audience and there wouldn't be much chance of that."

The audience was all too much in evidence. Across the street stood a row of the abandoned tenements. At every boarded-up doorway boards were being pushed aside and ragged squatters were coming out to inspect us. We had merely driven in and parked. Our inspection of the door and the lock had been quiet, but in no time at all we had drawn the onlookers.

One of them shouted from across the street.

"He ain't almost never there," he said. "Only a little time when he comes to bring some of his junk in or somebody comes and he has them take it away. He don't hang around none. Mostly it's just locked up and nobody here."

The inspector shouted back.

"Doesn't he have a watchman or somebody who stays around to mind the store?"

Four or five of them, including the one who had spoken, came across the street.

"He ain't got nobody," that one said.

They all nodded agreement and there was a chorus of mumbled "nobody."

"If he had a watchman," the inspector said, "maybe he wouldn't have burglars."

That drew him a laugh.

"Burglars? You know what he got in there? He got junk and it's junk nobody wants. Big junk. Heavy junk. Not like pipe or nothing you can sell. It's just junk junk."

"We heard he had burglars."

"Somebody been kidding you, mister. We know for sure. One of us or another, we're, somebody, here all the time. Everything goes on we see it."

"It was statues. Stone. A guy with a big sword, he's fighting a dragon."

For a moment I wondered how it could be that they seemed to be making no connection. It had been all over the newspapers and over and over again on the TV news spots. It was news. After all, death-by-dragon's-tail must eclipse man-bites-dog any day. Then it came to me. These were men who didn't see newspapers until they had picked up discarded ones. They had no television.

"Burglars got that?"

"That's what we were told."

"Bullshit."

"You know different?"

"We seen different. He was right here. It was like now, evening. A truck came and he was here like waiting for it. He helped bring them statues out and load them on the truck. He was all in a sweat the guy loading it on the truck would damage it maybe. The guy, he didn't give a shit. It's junk. It's already damaged and he's yelling and carrying on not to damage it."

"You saw the truck?"

"We seen it all."

"Did you notice the name on the truck? Do you remember what it was?"

"No name on the truck. Nothing."

Nudging the talkative man, another one of them stepped forward and took over.

"What do you want to know for? What's it to you?"

"Just curious," Schmitty said.

"You're too curious."

That was it. The one who had previously been doing all the talking got the message. The lot of them drifted back across the street and stood watching us from there. I tried to console the inspector.

"They gave you everything you need to know," I said. "You had it all before they clammed up."

"I would have liked a description of the careless trucker," Schmitty said.

"What I would like is for this to begin to make the first particle of sense," I said.

"We've got one liar identified."

"Does it do us any good?"

"Knowing this much, I can do a better job of leaning on Mr. André Bartholomew."

Back in the inspector's car we were heading west when a call came through on his car telephone. It was a report on Ethel Cameron. Schmitty took it with the telephone receiver wedged between his ear and his shoulder. Skewed that way in what I considered was no shape in which to be driving, instead of pulling into the curb until he had finished on the phone, the inspector stamped on the gas and had us hurtling through the streets at a pace that was nothing short of suicidal.

Even when he had finished with the call and was giving his full attention to his wild zigzag through traffic, I was determined to keep a tight rein on my curiosity. I wanted to wait till we had come to a stop. I was not about to risk diverting him with any questions. I might just as well have asked since he told me in any case.

"Ethel," he said. "She thought she was giving it the smart play, but it looks like she wasn't nearly smart enough. They never are. People who talk and talk too little, it's always happening to them."

"What's happened to her?" Since there was no stopping his talking, I was asking.

"Fractured left wrist, some broken ribs. She won't talk to anyone but me. She says she'll talk to me. She's anxious to talk to me."

"Where is she?"

"Hospital."

There was no need for him to name the hospital. I know the city. Just from the direction of our wild ride I knew where we were headed.

"Beaten up?"

"What else? If it was only a fall downstairs, she could talk about that to anybody. She wouldn't be yelling for Inspector Schmidt and nobody else."

"MacPherson?"

"Vice Squad has come through on MacPherson. It's Eloise MacPherson. She's off the street. Call girl, very high-class, very expensive."

"Cameron lives with her?"

"No. The way it looked, she didn't want us to know where she lived. Now I'm guessing it was rather that she didn't want to go home. She was afraid of this, afraid it would catch up with her there. She wasn't smart enough. It's caught up with her anyhow."

"She's going to tell you who?"

"Who is the least of it. That she doesn't have to tell me, not anymore."

"You know?"

"If you don't, you're not thinking."

I didn't have to think. He was back on the phone. I was wishing he wouldn't. I would have been happier if he had let it wait until we had pulled up at the hospital, but it was no good saying anything. He was putting the word out on Jocko. He wanted the bartender picked up.

"For now you can call it assault," he said.

Embarrassment took my mind off the continuing hazard of our insane ride. Of course, I hadn't been thinking. Nothing could have been more obvious. I had grooved myself so deeply in the notion that Jocko had come to talk to me and had been hanging about across the street from my place waiting till he could have me alone that, even when I had been asking myself who could have known she had gone to the police and how could anyone have known, I had not even then made the connection. Certainly the conclusion was inescapable. Jocko hadn't been hanging around to see me. He had been following Ethel.

"He was the one she saw carry me in off the street," I said.

There are two fairly uniform approaches used by pimps in punishing a girl. Which it will be depends on what future plans he might have for her. If the punishment is not directed toward her improvement but is meted out to serve as a warning to his other girls, then he will work on her face. He's going to dump her, but before he does, he destroys her looks.

If, however, he is going to keep her on, he is careful to keep her face undamaged. It is not in his interest to reduce her street value. On the basis of the list of injuries the inspector had recited to me I was ready to make a prediction on what Ethel Cameron would have to tell the inspector, this intelligence that she would impart only to him and to nobody else. She had made her sworn statement to him. She wanted to talk to him now, because now she was about to retract it.

I had the whole thing built in my mind. Just what the inspector had said she could tell to anyone she was saving to tell to him. Nobody had beaten her. She had just fallen downstairs. Lying there in her hospital bed, however, she'd had time to think and she was retracting everything she had given him in that statement she had signed and sworn. I was curious only to see how she was going to explain such a turnaround. I was convinced that it was to precisely such a turnaround that Inspector Schmidt was rushing us at the risk of our lives.

At first sight of her in her hospital bed, I was ready

to call the list of reported injuries significantly incomplete. Her face looked ravaged. It was now without even the smallest claim to prettiness. It was puffily swollen. The skin was blotched. She had a mean and angry look. All of this, however, I came to recognize, was only the secondary result of the beating she had taken.

Her face was in fact unmarked. The swelling had come from crying. The rest of it was only the manifestations of pain and of rage. Also hers was a face that may once have looked good enough without make-up. Now it looked not so much scrubbed as stripped. It was the eyebrows or more exactly the absence of them. They had been mercilessly plucked. Without the replacement afforded by eyebrow pencil she looked as though she had an ugly scar above each eye.

She stopped for not so much as a word of greeting or even long enough to listen to some sympathetic murmurings. She was talking even before we had settled at her bedside.

"They told you I got to talk to you," she said.

"I'm here," the inspector said. "I'm here to listen."

"Yeah. Listen and listen good. All that stuff I told you—I told you only because I was drunk. He got me drunk." With the arm she had free of a cast she made a sweeping gesture in my direction. She no more than began the gesture. With a gasp and a grimace of pain she quickly aborted it. Then, pulling herself together, she went on. "He didn't mean to get me drunk, but it was the champagne. I never had no champagne before."

"And now you're sobered up," the inspector said.

"You just ain't kidding," she said. "Now I know exactly what I am doing. I didn't let them give me any of that pain-killer stuff because maybe it would make me like drunk again. I wasn't going to have any of that without I'd talked to you first."

"Then let's do this quickly and not keep you too long from the pain-killers."

"Yeah. What I told you about seeing somebody carry him inside—I wasn't going to tell you that. If I wasn't drunk, I wouldn't have let anything slip out. But I was drunk and I slipped and then I had to tell you something."

"You want to change your statement?" the inspector asked. "The whole statement or that part of it only?"

I was still expecting a retraction. I thought she was taking a hopelessly clumsy way of going about it. I couldn't have been more off base.

"I'm not changing anything except I'm going to tell you what I was never going to tell. How do they say it? 'The truth, the whole truth, and nothing but the truth.' I told you the truth and nothing but the truth."

"And now it's going to be the whole truth?"

"Yeah. I said I couldn't see who it was carried him in off of the street. I saw and no mistake, but he'd been good to me and I thought I loved him. I was never going to tell on him. No way."

"Jocko," the inspector said.

"You knew?"

"He put you here. He beat up on you."

"He's an animal."

"He did this to you and now you're going to get even with him."

"He did this to me and now I know he's an animal. He's like a mad dog or something. He's got to be put away. You got to put him away, Inspector."

"Before he gives you a lot worse?"

"Yes. He told me it was going to be a lot worse. He told me I'd get it if I didn't take back everything I told you and if I didn't keep my mouth shut. Well, I can't keep my mouth shut—not about murder, I can't. He's your murderer, Inspector. You got to put him away."

"This is the wrong way to do it," Schmitty said. "You'll have to tell me exactly what you know, everything you know. Then I can take it from there. Just calling him a killer doesn't mean anything."

"I already told you. I seen him with Mr. Bagby up in his arms. I seen him carry Mr. Bagby inside. It was him and nobody else."

"Okay. I have that. What else did you see?"

"Nothing else. I saw that. Nothing else."

"The whole truth?"

"That's the whole truth, Inspector."

"It's something but it's not enough. On that and no more you're calling him a murderer?"

"On everything," she said, "on the whole thing."

It didn't come easily. Inspector Schmidt had to dig for it. For all his digging, however, he had from her not even one small additional fact. What she gave him was only an assemblage, the way she was putting together bits and pieces that we already knew.

There was Jocko's denial of my charge that he had given me a mickey. She had been believing that. In her experience she had seen too many guys who had taken that one drink too many.

"They was just like him, not good for anything except it was maybe for getting theirselves rolled."

She hadn't known that, when she had looked over from across the avenue, he had seen her and she had said nothing to him about having seen him. She had been putting only the best interpretation on what she'd seen. She'd been thinking that he had come out of the club to go home, had seen me passed out on the sidewalk and, worried about me out there in the weather, had carried me back into the club so I could sleep it off where I'd be warm and under cover.

"When I let it slip to you that I'd seen something," she said, "it was only the drunk way I was thinking. I was going to put in like a good word for Jocko. I was going to show you how he had a good heart. He wasn't the kind, he'd give anybody a mickey. Then right off I got to thinking how he said he wasn't even there that late, not after that Peters . . ."

"And you'd been thinking he'd told an innocent man's harmless lie," the inspector said, trying to help her along. "You thought he was just avoiding unjust suspicion and, thinking that, you had to back away from exposing him. And why not since you were sure it made no difference?"

"Yeah. Like that. You see how it was, Inspector. I wanted to help, but I thought that wouldn't be helping any. It would only be making trouble for Jocko."

"And now you do want to make trouble for him," Schmitty said.

"Now I know it wasn't like I thought."

"How do you know? That's what you have to tell me. How do you know?"

She touched the cast on her wrist and she touched her side.

"I got plenty here and it's telling me," she said. "You know how he did it? He knocked me down and he stood over me and kicked me. He kicked and he kicked, and it wasn't like he was crazy mad. He was cold and he was like teaching me. You know what I mean?"

"And he taught you to stop loving him," the inspector said.

"He taught me a lot more than that. He taught me what he was. We've been a long time, him and me, and it ain't like I never before done anything to make him mad. So he'd yell at me, but he never once raised a hand to me. So what is it now? What did I do it's so terrible? It's so terrible only because he's the one. He's the murderer."

It was reasonable enough within the limits of what she could know but only within those limits. There remained the question of André Bartholomew and the impossible burglary story he'd been feeding the inspector. Schmitty didn't bring that up. There would have been no point to it. She couldn't have been expected to contribute anything in that area. Instead Schmitty went probing after a motive.

"Tell me about Jocko," he said. "Does he have any other girls?"

"How do you mean?"

"Call girls? Girls he has out on the street?"

"He's a bartender," she said.

"With a sideline. The street out in front of the club, it's been your territory. Who gave it to you?"

"Nobody gave it to me."

"Oh, come on, Ethel!"

"Well, Jocko, but not like you think."

"How not?"

"He never took anything off of me like they do when they're in it like a business. When we was together, him and me, it was for love. So anybody came in and tried to crowd me, he pushed them off."

"Eloise MacPherson?"

"She's my friend. She don't have nothing to do with him."

"You went to her place. Did he just happen to catch up with you there or did she perhaps tip him?"

"It wasn't like that. It wasn't up at her place. It was later, when I went home."

She explained that. Going to her friend's apartment had been a move made only so she could shed us.

"I didn't want him knowing I'd been to the cops," she said. "You bring me home to my place and he maybe sees you, he'd know. So I gave you the other address and once you'd dropped me and gone off, I just went home. He was there in my place, waiting for me, and he knew." She fell silent for a moment or two, brooding. When she spoke again, it was with fresh and other-directed anger. "I could have known he'd get told," she said. "Some smart-ass cop seen me downtown and quick like a bunny he goes tell Jocko. Bartenders, they all got them friends on the cops."

I had been keeping out of it, but on that I had to speak. I told her how it had been. Jocko had needed no informant. It did nothing to change her opinion of police officers. It just made her resentful of me. I had known he had seen her with me and I hadn't told her. She had expected better of me.

The inspector broke in on that. "You were thinking he wasn't the killer," he said. "You were lying for him, trying to protect him. Why didn't you want him to know you had been talking to me and making that big pitch for him?"

"I made that one slip. I said I seen somebody. If you was going to ask me was it Jocko, and it had to be sooner or later you would be asking me, I was going to swear up and down it wasn't him. I was going to tell you that if it was him, I'd have known him. I was going to swear it was somebody else and I didn't know who."

"Then he beat up on you because you'd said too much and he thought it was the way to make sure you wouldn't say any more?"

"I swore I hadn't told on him."

"But he didn't believe you?"

"He believed me. If he didn't believe me, he'd have killed me or anyway spoiled my face. This was just for talking to you at all. If I told on him, I'd get worse."

"And now you're telling."

"Of course, I'm telling," she said. Then she lapsed into some homespun psychology. "Men," she said. "They're so damn sure they can do anything with muscle that they never think. Just because they don't think, they don't know that another person will. Us women, we're different. We think. We've got to. They've got us outmuscled. If we never got them outthunk, we'd all be like slaves, not that a lot of us ain't."

"One more question," the inspector said.

"All the questions you want. I already told you everything I know, but if you think there's maybe more, it could be and I ain't thunk of it."

"You didn't want to have anything to do with Peters. You knew too much about him. How did you know? Had you ever?"

"With him? No. Never with him."

"Then how did you know?"

"I heard around."

"Around isn't enough. From someone. Who?"

"There's a girl in the show. She's one of them they

call the Towers. You know what they're like, big and husky and strong, like them women out of East Germany or Russia they get in the Olympics. Any one of them, she'd make two of me. What he done to that girl —I should try to tangle with him?"

"Did she tell you?"

"No. I only heard."

"From who?"

"Jocko. He tips me to some guy is going to be good. Other guys he warns me off of, like he can tell they're going to be tightwads or even they're kinkies."

"How did he know?"

"A girl she's in the club—how wouldn't he know?"

"Just a girl in the club? Not his girl?"

"I was his girl."

"Always been?"

"A long time now, long before that big Tower dope ever came off of the farm."

"So, when she came along, you were already his girl. Are you sure he wasn't having something on the side?"

"With her? If he was, he'd be mashed flatter even than that Peters was."

"You'd do that?"

"Me? Me like swing on Jocko? You think I'm crazy?"

"A heavy block of stone dropped on him from a high place?"

"I'd have to have me the stone and a high place and him waiting underneath. I didn't mean me. She's got her a man. That Rich Dawson. He's hardly like a man. He's more like maybe some grizzly bear."

"Dawson didn't come into it until after Peters had done his number on her, but he's been wanting the creep's hide and wanting it bad. We know that. How do they get along, the two of them, Jocko and Dawson?"

"They don't."

"Anything that would make Jocko do Dawson any favors?"

"Jocko? He don't do nobody favors. Least of all Rich Dawson. Jocko thinks he's a lot of man. Rich Dawson don't help him think it and Jocko hates that. There's two people I know he hates and it's both for the same reason. One of them's Dawson."

"The other one?"

"The Face."

"That little guy?"

"Little guy with the big brain. Dawson makes Jocko feel small just looking at him. The Face he does it too, except with him it's his tongue."

"Where does Jocko hang out when he isn't home or working in the club?"

"My place."

"Last night?"

"No."

"He didn't go home last night."

"Nights when he don't go home, he goes to my place."

"And if the next day is his day off, he goes home in the day and sleeps."

"I suppose. I know he does a lot of sleeping."

"Not today. Today if he did, it wasn't in his place."

"Today seems he was following me around, spying on me and I don't know what else. What do guys do the next day after they killed somebody?"

CHAPTER 9

On our way out we paused at the nursing station to tell them that their patient now wanted the sedation she had up to that time been refusing.

"She kept herself clearheaded," I said, as we were leaving the hospital. "She makes good sense. All it leaves for you is finding André Bartholomew's place in the picture."

"She has a hurt wrist, hurt ribs, and hurt feelings," Schmitty said. "She was taking all her pain full strength and pain doesn't necessarily contribute to clear thinking. It's great, though, for keeping anger from simmering down."

"You don't believe her?"

"Truth, whole truth, and nothing but the truth? Yes. There could be only one reason for doubting her now that she's made her story complete and that would have been only if a suspicion that she might herself have been the killer could be made to stand up. It can't."

"I could never believe it," I said, "but that's emotional. When I was sitting on the sidewalk, I formed a picture of her that made her a kind and considerate person. I'm grooved in that feeling about her, but intellectually . . . ?"

"Intellectually you'd have to find some logic for anybody laying that beating on her," Schmitty said. "'You killed a creep, you naughty girl. I'm going to have to punish you for that.' Intellectually, Baggy, can you go along with believing anything like that? Of course you can't. It has to be that somebody took the wrong way of trying to silence her. So who would bother if he wasn't guilty?"

"So it is Jocko?"

"So she has all those good, get-even reasons for thinking it's Jocko. I'm believing her facts, but we must keep an open mind about her assumptions and her conclusions. You can't call her unbiased."

"But you just asked the question yourself. Who would bother if he wasn't guilty?"

"Yes. But there's still the question of guilty of what," the inspector said. "Also we must ask guilty to what degree. Accessory could be enough, even if it was unwitting accessory."

"He didn't know he was feeding me a mickey?"

"It's possible that he didn't know why. On what you've told me, he was given to following orders. It could have been an order he liked."

"The Face's orders. He was just following orders but then he found that he had contributed to a murder. So now everything is going to hang on breaking down The Face's alibi. If that holds, you're left with Jocko."

"Not that simple," Schmitty said. "All his alibi witnesses are his good friends. They won't be changing their story. If it's Drew, I'll be needing some other evidence, something that will make that heavily corroborated alibi of his worthless. If it's Jocko, I'll need more evidence before I can pin it on him."

"Either way," I asked, "where do you go for the additional evidence?"

"For starters to a phone book."

He parked in front of a drugstore. It was a big store with a battery of phone booths at the back. Alongside the booths there was a full array of directories, the complete set for all of the five boroughs. He took the Manhattan book and flipped to the *B*s.

"Bartholomew?"

"Home address."

I was looking over his shoulder. There was only one listing for "Bartholomew, André. Architectural Ornaments." It was the address Schmitty already had, the business premises. There were no listings under Bartholomew, A. The inspector set the Manhattan book aside and reached for Brooklyn.

I took Queens. We drew simultaneous blanks. There was no address for him in either borough. So then it was the Bronx for the inspector and Staten Island for me. Neither of us came up with anything.

"No home phone," I said, "or else it must be an unlisted number."

"Unlisted number," the inspector said. "Everybody has a phone and I can't see Bartholomew as a commuter type."

"He has the answering service," I said. "He can be depending on them to cover personal calls as well as business."

"Could be, but do you know anybody nowadays who lives in a place where he can't call out?"

"Hotel?"

"Cheap rent for the business and spare no expense for himself? Not likely."

We were back in the car and, so far as I could determine, we were backtracking on the route we had taken to the hospital. I couldn't see where there would be anything gained from returning to the warehouse, but we were headed in that direction. Since it seemed impossible that it wouldn't be some other destination Inspector Schmidt had in mind, I was waiting to see where he would turn off. He didn't, but he went only as far as the outer rim of that derelict neighborhood. He pulled up at the local precinct station house.

The precinct captain wasn't there. There has to be something important going on in his part of town for a precinct captain to work a night or an evening shift. Asking for him was no more than a protocol gesture. Schmitty had expected that he would be settling for a lieutenant. He satisfied himself with that.

I was recalling times when he had expressed himself on the subject. You can't simply bypass the man in command. That's bad for departmental discipline. If you're lucky, however, you'll get to work with one of the younger men, a cop who's still on the way up.

"The higher we go," he would say, including even himself of whom it was conspicuously untrue, "the less we know and the stupider we get. If you want somebody sharp, you need a kid who's still getting it made."

"André Bartholomew," Schmitty said.

"Andy B.," the lieutenant said. "That one, Inspector, is our precinct pain in the ass. Every station house has one and Andy B. is ours."

"Specify, Lieutenant."

"You can count on Andy B. for one complaint a day and two on Sundays. The trouble with him is he's right and you can't tell him he isn't. He's right and he's unreasonable about it. That's the unbeatable combination."

"What kind of complaints?"

"Just the one, but always over and over. He never gives up. He's got this old warehouse."

"We've been over there."

"Then you know it's not Madison Avenue, never anything like. He wants it to be."

"And you call that unreasonable. I'll go along with you there. What does he want you to do?"

"Those condemned tenements down that way, they're full of winos, bag ladies, bums. He keeps demanding that we get them out and keep them out. He complains that they make a bad impression on his customers."

"They're over there now," the inspector said.

"They are, Inspector, and they shouldn't be. Don't we just know it? The law says they should be out. Their having no place else to go says they should be in. All I know is that it's out and back in, out and back in. Bartholomew comes around here screaming and we hit a day when there's not so much hell breaking loose that we can't spare a few men. So we do a sweep. We can't do the whole neighborhood. That would take an army, but we do his block. We get them out and they drift right back in again. We can't spare the men day after day every day to keep the block patrolled."

"Then he complains again."

"You'd think he'd get to see how it's no use, but he's on our backs all the time. We're hoping around here that things may possibly get better now that we have something on Mr. The-Law-Is-The-Law Andy B."

"Something on him?" the inspector asked. "Something like what?"

"We've been hearing that he's in financial trouble, way behind on his rent, eviction coming up. So now he's yelling burglary."

"Is he? When he was talking to me, he said he

couldn't be bothered reporting it. He said we never recover anybody's stolen property."

The lieutenant worked up a wry grin. "That's our Andy B. again," he said. "Always right and never ready to be reasonable about it."

It was the lieutenant's idea that Bartholomew would be trying to work himself out of his financial bind by putting in a phony insurance claim.

"He sold someone that dragon thing and now he can say it wasn't sold. It was stolen. His customer used it to kill that guy in the nightclub alley. The world's smartest insurance investigator isn't going to be able to find that guy and persuade him to say he bought the thing and paid for it. He'll be saying he never had it. If he ever gets found, at least, that'll be what he'll be saying."

"Bartholomew has this place and nobody there most of the time. He has no night watchman and he says he's not there much himself. If something goes wrong over there, have you a number where you can reach him?"

"Let me check the file, Inspector."

He came back with a phone number and an address. The inspector made a note of both. The address was in Greenwich Village. You could say it was at the edge of the Village. More properly it was in a nondescript area into which the Village had been expanding. I knew those streets and essentially they were not much different from the area in which the man had his warehouse.

The difference was that the old tenements down there, because of their proximity to the Village, had been picked up short of the drop into terminal decay. They had been given a patch job and cosmetic treatment. That ran to coats of pink or lavender paint to cover the grimy brickwork. They were, therefore, occupied not by squatters but by people who would be paying such a rent as may well have been hurrying André Bartholomew into bankruptcy.

Riding down to the Village, I did some thinking aloud. "He's been in need of money," I said. "He could have been bought."

"It's one possibility," the inspector said.

"That or the fake insurance claim?"

"No. He's not that stupid. Putting in an insurance claim for a burglary on which he hasn't established any kind of a police record—that can bring him nothing but trouble. He can't be so dumb that he wouldn't know that much."

"Other possibility then? That he's your man?"

"Not likely. The argument Drew gave us for himself might be even stronger for Bartholomew. A prize piece, which he is holding for a high price, isn't something he's going to waste when there's all that other less valuable junk that would do the job as well."

"And just as The Face used it to argue his innocence, Bartholomew could have chosen it for the same reason, to make it a killing that would appear to be out of character for him. What's wrong with that?"

"It could be," Schmitty said. "It's a little far out, but it could be."

"Still not the other possibility you have in mind?" I asked.

"I'm wondering whether Andy B. mightn't be telling the truth and it was a burglary."

"Out of that fortress?"

"There can always be a key job."

"And no report to the police and no change of lock. That's an old lock he has on the door."

"You don't have to change the whole lock. You can just have the cylinders changed. I'll be asking him about that. I'd like to see a receipted bill from a locksmith."

"What about all those people who saw him load it on the truck?" I asked.

Schmitty grimaced. "I could like that a lot better," he said, "if the lieutenant hadn't kicked a hole into their credibility."

"He'll claim malice on their part."

"What else? No question that there was malice. You could smell it on them."

"Was that what I was smelling?" I said. "I thought it was just that they hadn't bathed."

At the Bartholomew home address we found just about what I'd expected. The grimy brickwork had been painted yellow and the yellow was in turn begrimed. The front door had a gleaming coat of vermilion paint, but the steps that led up to it were chipped.

The inspector checked the vestibule bells and letter boxes. None was marked for André Bartholomew or for any other Bartholomew.

"Flat shared with someone else and the other person's name on the box and the bell," I said. "Could be the same with the phone, not an unlisted number but just listed under the other name."

"Could be, but then you usually have both names on the bell and the letter box. Extra name listed in the phone book puts an extra charge on the bill. Extra name on the bell here is for free."

On the evidence of the bells and the letter boxes at least half of the flats in the building were shared. They were marked with two names and in one case even three.

"Want me to flip a coin for which you'll try first?" I offered.

"That can wait."

The inspector was pulling out of the vestibule. He had the home phone number. I assumed he was about to resort to that. At the foot of the front steps, however, he turned and took the three steps that led down to the basement. There was a separate bell and letter box by the basement door, but there was no need to check on how they were marked.

That basement door was framed by a pair of delicately fluted colonnettes that could never have been a part of the original structure and above the door was a fanlight that had never been planned for even the most fancily converted tenement basement. It spoke only of gracious living in an Edith Wharton or Henry James New York. The fanlight showed a pleasant yellow glow. No light was showing through the basement windows. The inspector rang the bell. When there was no response, he tried again. This time he leaned on it.

That brought a bellow from inside.

"Whatever it is, I don't want any. Go away."

Schmitty brought his finger back to the bell and kept it there. After several moments the door banged open and Bartholomew loomed in the doorway. He was brandishing an iron bar. Since this was André Bartholomew, it was perhaps inevitable that it should be a wrought-iron bar entwined in wrought-iron ivy. In this situation, however, it didn't look like what it was. It looked like one of the nastier weapons out of the tenth century.

"Put it away," the inspector said. "You're giving yourself a bad image."

Bartholomew kept his hold on the bar, but now he was only holding it. He wasn't brandishing it.

"You," he said. "I told you everything. Haven't you anything better to do than going through all that again?"

"Nothing better, Mr. Bartholomew, now that I have witnesses to say that you're a liar."

"What witnesses?"

He put explosive emphasis on the "what," giving it a lot of breath. The breath came at us. It had so much whiskey on it that I could almost have named the brand.

"I suggest we take this inside, unless you're so hooked on witnesses that you want to attract crowds of them."

Bartholomew took a step back, giving us room to come through.

"You're going to interfere with my drinking," he said.

"Jail does that," the inspector said.

Bartholomew had a little time for giving thought to the inspector's words. Before leading us into his big front room, he made a big deal out of the care with which he set down the piece of wrought iron he had been brandishing.

In the room I could see why his windows had been showing no light. They were covered with mahogany shutters, and those were only a part of what had obviously been the salvage from some fine old house. The fireplace and mantel were carved marble with a row of fat cherubs supporting the mantel.

The rest of the room was reminiscent of The Face's private quarters in those rooms above The Topless

Towers. Here, however, capitals, column bases, and
column drums had all been pressed into use. Topped
with slabs of marble or sheets of glass they had been
made into tables.

From one of the glass tops he picked up a drink he
had been working on. From the color of its contents it
was obviously overwhelmingly more whiskey than
water. He disposed of it in a series of long gulps. Only
when it was empty did he set it aside and turn to the
inspector.

"What witnesses?" he repeated.

"Your neighbors uptown who watched you help with
the loading of the St. George and the dragon. If that
was a burglary, they're saying you assisted in it."

"Them. I might have known. If you don't know it, I
can tell you. Nobody's going to believe a word they
say, not that scum, never."

"Because they're down on their luck?"

"Because they're scum. Because they have no right
to be there. Because I've been trying to get you people
to root them out of there. I've been trying without success, but I have been trying and they know it. They
hate me."

"There are some facts that give them credibility."

"What facts?"

"No signs of breaking and entering. Those are strong
bars on the windows. That's a terrific door and a
terrific lock."

"I never said it was a break-in."

"Key job?"

"Obviously."

"You haven't changed the lock. Have a cylinder job
done on it?"

"Lock the door after the horse is stolen?"

Inspector Schmidt raised his eyebrows. "That big a job?" he asked. "Cleaned you out completely? You have nothing left to go on with?"

"Nothing of value. I never have that much good stuff around. Good pieces go almost as fast as I get them. The St. George was the only thing I had that was worth anything much. With that gone I won't be worrying until the next time I've picked up something good."

"Drew wants to sell. If you're down to nothing, why aren't you buying?"

"He's a clown and he's crazy. Everything he's got—he's offering all or nothing. Sure, he's got a lot of good stuff, but there's also a lot of the junk I'm overloaded with already. I'll take the trash to get his good stuff but first he's going to have to get to be more realistic about price. He's not even talking about just getting the money back and on the trash even that would be ridiculous. He's looking for a profit on every last piece. So if there was to be anything in it for me, I'd have to ask crazy prices. You can't do business that way, not if you want to stay in business."

"Don't people who collect stuff expect it to appreciate in value?" Schmitty asked.

"They expect. There's no limit to what crazies can expect. There is a limit to what they can get." His lips were twitching. He tried to suppress it, but it got away from him. He broke out in a guffaw. "A crazy like Drew," he said between barks of laughter, "he never has enough of anything. He's not selective. He buys everything. He wants everything. You get someone like him and you stick him but good. There isn't a thing he ever got from me where he didn't overpay. That collection of his will have to do a lot of appreciating before it even begins to be worth what he paid for it."

"That's the way you do business? Anytime you land a sucker, you shaft him?"

"Buying cheap and selling high. Any other way to do business, Inspector?"

"Giving fair value and taking a decent profit."

"Nice guys go into bankruptcy," Bartholomew said.

"So how did you manage to come so close?" Schmitty asked.

"Close to what?"

"To bankruptcy."

"I'm all right."

"Are you? Okay. You overcharge when you can. Somebody comes to you and you make a good, fat sale. A condition of the sale is that you never reveal the name of the buyer, not to anyone and that is to include the police. What kind of a percentage would a condition of that sort add to your profit?"

"Academic question, Inspector," Bartholomew said, pouring himself a fresh drink. My estimate of proportion of water to whiskey was verified. He made no move to offer us any. I suppose he was tacitly telling us that we were not guests. "I run a legitimate business. I would never enter into a deal under such conditions."

The inspector forged ahead, pretending that the denial had never been made.

"At the point that you got to know why the condition had been made," he said, "and it became obvious that sooner or later there would be police questions about the sale, you couldn't feel comfortable about merely refusing to name the buyer. You weren't certain that you couldn't be forced to name him. You got the notion that it would be safer to call it a burglary."

"If you choose to believe that," Bartholomew said, "there's nothing I can do about it. I certainly am not about to invent a fantasy that will be in accord with your insane notions."

"That burglary bit was a spur-of-the-moment idea," Schmitty said. "Lies are likely to be not much good unless they're prepared lies. You made no preparations, mister. You laid no groundwork. A report to the police, a change in the lock cylinder, and an insurance claim would have been all it would have taken."

"It's natural that you should know more about such things than I ever could," Bartholomew said. "I run a clean, honest . . ."

He was asserting his probity, but he left the assertion unfinished. A ring of his doorbell interrupted him, and he froze. It wasn't any ordinary ring. It had the sound of a signal. It was a quick succession of rings, a little rhythmic phrase in a tum-ti-tum-ti-tum-tum pattern.

Bartholomew was making no move toward answering it. The inspector started toward the door. Bartholomew did a quick jump to place himself in Inspector Schmidt's path.

"I know who it is," he said. "He's a nuisance. Ignore him and he'll go away."

The inspector started to walk around the man.

"I can send him away if I don't want to ask him in," Schmitty said.

Bartholomew grabbed at his arm. "Don't do that to me," he said. "Once he's in here, I'll be stuck with him. I'll have hell's own time getting rid of him."

He was addressing the last of that to the inspector's back. Schmitty wasn't listening.

Bartholomew's voice broke like a teenager's. It went shrill. The man was bleating.

"This is my house. I've got rights. I've got a say about who comes in here and who doesn't."

The inspector was out to the door. He turned the knob, and he had no more than started to pull it open when the door came at him with so much force that it all but knocked him backward. I read it for someone who had expected the door to be slammed in his face and had come prepared to force his way in.

I was misreading it. As the door shot open, a body that had been propped against it fell across the threshold, striking against the inspector's legs. Jumping back, Schmitty disengaged himself from it. He rammed it to one side of the doorway and edged past it to dash out to the street. As best I could, I followed after him.

The street was empty. Nothing showed anywhere, not the taillights of a fleeing car, not a face at any window. Muttering curses, Inspector Schmidt headed back. Sobbing and moaning, Bartholomew was bent over in the doorway working at the body. He was doing none of the things that should have been done. He was just shoving it away from his door.

As we came back in, he had just pushed it clear. Straightening up, he tried to slam the door shut. In his gibbering hysteria he was fumbling. Inspector Schmidt was not. Lunging at the closing door, the inspector slammed his shoulder into it. The door flew open and knocked Bartholomew to the floor. The man just sat there, blubbering.

Planted in the doorway, the inspector now took his

turn at bending over the body. It was Jocko and he was dead. A fusillade of bullets had come close to cutting him in two. Talking across the body that lay between them, Schmitty spoke to Bartholomew.

"Now you've got a nuisance that isn't going to go away," he said.

Bartholomew made a great effort to pull himself together.

"Who is he?"

"You don't know?"

"He's dead, isn't he?"

"He's dead. Take a good look at him."

"I've seen him."

"Nobody you know?"

"How would I know him?"

"He's been delivered to you. Somebody expects you to be interested."

"I'm not interested."

"He's here."

"And you're going to ask me why? Dammit. I don't know why."

"Who rang the bell?"

"How would I know? It wasn't this man. It couldn't have been, I suppose."

"You're right. It couldn't have been. He was too dead."

"And there was nobody else at the door. So how can I know?"

"You said you knew who it was. You knew the ring. You said he was a nuisance and he would go away. You couldn't have been more right about that and on both counts. You know him, and when a man makes this kind of delivery, I'll have to know his name."

"I didn't know who it was. I just said that because I

didn't want anybody coming in. I was being questioned by the police. Would I have wanted anybody to know that? It would have been all over the neighborhood in no time. The way people gossip, I would never have heard the end of it."

CHAPTER 10

That the man had never shown any great competence as a liar you already know. Reduced to gibbering hysteria, he was beyond anything more than just reaching for words. He was in no shape for making judgments on the ones he chose. He may have been hoping for credibility, but he was relying on nothing more than vehemence.

Inspector Schmidt chose to use the phone in his car. Going inside to Bartholomew's telephone would have taken him away from Jocko's body. Until he could have reinforcements to take over on the corpse he was not letting it out of his sight. I stayed in the doorway with Bartholomew, watching him work at getting a grip on himself. He brought the sobs under control and he stilled the blubbering, but it was obvious that he hadn't calmed down. He got the shakes. They were not only visible. They were audible as well. I could hear the chattering of his teeth.

Speech came only in broken measures. I was listening carefully in the event that there might be something I would need to relay to the inspector, but it was only the same thing over and over. He didn't want the body left where it was. He wanted to know if the inspector was arranging for its removal. If he wasn't, then when would he?

"He can't just leave it here," he kept saying. "I can't even close the door."

It was an exaggeration since, before the inspector had stopped him, he had already shoved the body clear of the door. In any event closing the door would most certainly have been the least of his problems. Going on and on about it, however, seemed to be his shield against trying to cope with anything more important. I was keeping a close watch on him against the possibility that he might undertake to deal with the body himself.

I soon came to see, however, that it was unnecessary. He made no move toward it. He was, in fact, shrinking back from it, putting between the body and himself as much space as was possible in the narrow confines of the vestibule.

Finishing with his telephone call, Inspector Schmidt came back to stand over the body. Bartholomew screamed at him.

"Are you just going to leave it there? When are you going to take it away?"

"In good time," Schmitty said. "When it's ready to be moved."

"It'll never be more ready. It's dead."

"Let's say when you have been looking at it long enough to understand that it can happen to you. You can't ignore that. You're likely to be next."

"Why me?"

"For the same reason as it happened to him," Schmitty said, "and for the same reason as delivered it to your door. It's what you know and it's the company you've been keeping, dangerous knowledge and dangerous company."

"I haven't been keeping any company. I've never seen him before. I don't even know who he is."

"They call him Jocko. He was the bartender at The Topless Towers."

"Drew's place? I've never been there."

"Hold it," Schmitty said. "You're talking to me, Inspector Schmidt. It was where you and I first met. Your memory can't be that bad."

"Upstairs in the back. Never in the club."

Talk stopped for a moment or two while the three of us just listened to the growing yowl of the police sirens. The contingent from the local precinct was the first to arrive. Theirs was the first response to the inspector's call. They had the shortest distance to come.

Schmitty turned it over to them. They could handle it for the few minutes before the men from his Homicide Squad would come on the scene. The photographing, measuring, and close examination would be for them. It would only be when they had finished with it that the body could be removed and carted off to the medical examiner.

Schmitty took Bartholomew back inside. Bartholomew was torn. Making only that small move, since it would relieve him of having to look longer at the body, was obviously welcome. Surrendering to the thought that it would lie where it had fallen for some indeterminate time was evidently something he couldn't stomach. He hung back for a moment.

"You can't leave the door open that way," he said.

"For the present it will have to stay open."

"But it's winter. I'll freeze."

"You can put a coat on. Anyhow it won't be for long. I'll be taking you downtown."

"What's downtown?"

"Police headquarters. Detention cells."

"You can't arrest me. You have no reason."

"Let's not rush anything," the inspector said. "I'll be taking you in for questioning. What happens after that will depend on your answers. I'd like it to be that we will be holding you for your protection."

"Protection from what?"

"That's what you are going to tell me. For now it's from whatever it is you're afraid of."

"I'm not afraid of anything."

"What's making you shake then? Malaria?"

"What makes me shake? That thing in my doorway. Wouldn't that make anybody shake? Anyhow I'm cold. The door open. Middle of winter."

"We're having a mild winter and you won't be cold for long. Down at headquarters we have the heat on and it's plenty of heat."

That could have been taken as a promise or as a threat. Bartholomew took it as a threat.

"You can't do anything to me," he said. "I'm calling my lawyer."

"If you think you need him," Schmitty said. "I'm not going to tell you you don't. You're the best judge of that."

"What is that supposed to mean?"

"If you have done anything that puts you in danger of the law, you can use a lawyer. If you haven't, you should be thinking that your lawyer won't be any good for protecting you from that nuisance who rang your bell and went away. You've seen what he left for you. I don't have to tell you that he's a dangerous nuisance."

"Somebody's framing me for something I don't even know anything about. I need a lawyer to help me establish my innocence."

"You don't have to establish your innocence. If anything concerning you is going to be established, it will be by me. That's my job, establishing guilt."

"When a man is innocent?"

"I like to think I'll be getting the right man," the inspector said. "For that I can use your help. If you are what you say you are, that's all I'll ever want from you, your help."

The inspector's Homicide men and the forensic specialists arrived. Bartholomew headed for the phone to make the call to his attorney. Schmitty stopped him long enough to tell him that it would be within a matter of only minutes that we would be making the move downtown. He suggested that Bartholomew have his lawyer meet him at headquarters.

He had no thanks for the suggestion. It may well have been that the man didn't realize that the inspector was giving him every break. Schmitty could have been moving him around to prolong the time before his lawyer could catch up with him. It has been done.

After making his call, Bartholomew started for one of the back rooms. The inspector was out at the door, but he had detailed a precinct officer to keep an eye on Bartholomew. When the officer moved to follow him, Bartholomew protested.

"Am I under arrest?" He demanded to know.

"No," the cop said, "but it's my orders."

"To follow me everywhere? To give me no privacy? Even in the john?"

"Yeah. But my orders don't say I've got to look at it."

Bartholomew left the front room and the cop went with him. They were gone only briefly. When they returned, the cop was grinning. Bartholomew had put on a huge padded coat, but he hadn't stopped with that.

He was giving it the full treatment—furry earmuffs, fur-lined mittens, and fur-lined snow boots. The winter up to that time had been snowless and nobody could remember when New York had last had as mild a January. Bartholomew was dramatizing his outrage over the open door. He had accoutred himself for riding down to headquarters as if behind a team of sledge dogs. The cop caught my eye. I counterfeited a fit of coughing in an effort to mask a guffaw. Bartholomew was quick to pick up on that.

"See?" he said. "That door standing open. We'll catch our deaths, the lot of us."

Schmitty came in and caught that. "We'll have the car heater on," he said, "and then I can be accused of sweating you. Let's go."

Bartholomew hung back. "You haven't read me my rights," he said. "My lawyer said you have to read me my rights."

"If you think you'll need them, I'll do it in the car."

"And you can't make me say anything till I have my lawyer with me."

"That's right and I also don't have to take you in. I can just go away and leave you. You'll be safe enough for a while. That'll be until the boys take the body away. I'll have to come back, of course, but since you seem to live alone here, that may not be for days— when the neighbors begin to notice the smell. Nice and warm the way you are in your coat and earmuffs and mittens and fur boots, it'll be speeded up."

Bartholomew made a great try at pretending that he was disregarding what the inspector had said. Whether it scared him into compliance, however, or he was just bowing to the unavoidable I had no way of knowing.

Either way it took nothing more to make him come along. He did, however, make one demand.

"You're not going to take me past that thing," he said.

"Is there another way?"

"Upstairs and out by the front steps."

"If what you've already seen of it won't loosen your tongue," Schmitty said, "another exposure isn't likely to help. So upstairs. Lead the way."

On the way down to headquarters Bartholomew gave out with nothing more articulate than moans and sighs. Inspector Schmidt did all the talking and there was no change in that until we had met up with Bartholomew's attorney and the two of them had had the demanded huddle. On the advice of counsel the man finally talked.

Making a statement under oath, he retreated from his unsworn assertion that the St. George and the dragon had been stolen out of his warehouse and that he knew nothing. His replacement for this fiction, however, seemed to me to be no more helpful. I was ready to call it a new fiction; but, true or false, I could see no way that it could be of any help.

"It wasn't stolen," he said. "I sold it. I was hard up for cash and I got a good price for it. It was to be a present and a surprise. So a condition of the sale was that I was to say nothing about it."

"Okay. Who bought it and who was to be surprised?"

"Paul Peters bought it and he wanted it delivered without Drew knowing it had come in."

"And when Peters had died of it, why all the secrecy then?"

"It was murder and I really had nothing to do with

it. I just thought I could stay out of it, not get mixed up in anything I didn't know and couldn't understand. I was frightened."

"Frightened of whom?"

"I didn't know. I don't know now. Somebody killed Peters and he did it by dropping that thing on him. I couldn't help thinking that at work and at home, everywhere, all the time, I am surrounded by things like that. I just wanted to keep quiet and not get anyone mad. I didn't want anything dropping on me."

"You had your delivery instructions from Peters?"

"Yes. He was the buyer."

"He told you to deliver it and take it up to the roof?"

"No. He just said I had to get it in there without Drew seeing it. It was to be a surprise."

"Then whose idea was it to leave it on the roof?"

"Nobody's."

"Yours?"

"Not even mine, really. It was just that there was no other place I could put it. All the upstairs rooms were locked. That left Drew's backstage dressing room and in there he'd see it right off. It would have been there or in the backstage corridor which would have been worse. I was thinking it was just as well that it had to be the roof since Drew didn't go up there often and it offered the best chance that Drew wouldn't see it before Peters would be springing his surprise. I didn't know how long that was going to be before he would be doing it."

"You wanted to stay uninvolved," the inspector said. "You didn't want anything dropping on you. The thing had belonged to you. It had come out of your place. How did your story that it had been stolen leave you less involved than the simple truth? You sold it to the man. That was your last connection with it. Afterward somebody dropped it on him and killed him. How could that involve you?"

"It couldn't," Bartholomew said. "But killers, people like that, I don't know what makes them tick. I don't know how their minds work. You tell me, Inspector. You're the expert, not me."

"Jocko's body dumped on your doorstep. Tell me what was that for?"

"I don't know. You were there. I can only guess they thought they could stop me telling you what I knew, scare me out of talking to you."

"Exactly. So now what do you know that they don't want you telling me?"

"Nothing, only what I just told you."

"That you sold the murder weapon to Peters and you put it up on the roof where it would be handiest to use?"

"You're twisting my words. That isn't what I said. I sold the St. George group to Peters. I delivered it according to his instructions, keeping it secret from Drew, and I put it the only place where I could."

"There could be nobody who would be wanting you not to say that unless it was Peters and Peters is dead. There has to be something more that you aren't telling me."

"There isn't anything more. I don't know anything more. I've told you everything."

"Then why is Jocko dead on your doorstep?"

"They must be thinking I know more than I know. They must be thinking there is something I could tell you when there's just nothing."

" 'They,' " the inspector said. "You keep saying 'they.' Who are 'they'?"

"I don't know. How would I know?"

"Who's been threatening you? Who's been forcing you to lie to me?"

"Nobody. I'm not lying to you. I've told you everything I know. I'm swearing to it."

"Let's try this another way then. You delivered the thing and you took it up to the roof where you left it. You didn't do that alone. Who was your helper?"

"I did it alone."

"Your neighbors aren't saying that you loaded it on the truck and drove it away. They say you helped load it on the truck."

"Them. You can't believe a word they say."

"The funny thing is that I can," Schmitty said. "They have it in for you. If they can say anything to get you in trouble, they'll say it, no matter that it might be untrue. The hitch is how could they possibly know that saying there was someone else with you loading the truck would be a thing that could get you in trouble?"

"People like that, I don't know what they could think."

This was an obvious refuge—his ignorance of the thought processes of murderers and now of the indigent.

"It was a lot of weight for any one man to handle."

"Not doing it one piece at a time. It's all in pieces that fit together. One piece at a time, it can be handled."

He was on safe ground there. The thing was in sections and no one piece of it weighed more than one strong man could lift and carry. After all, it had been just the one piece of it, the dragon's tail, that had been lifted over the parapet and dropped on Peters in the alley.

"You're leaving yourself as the only one of whom we can say certainly that you knew where it was when it came time to use it."

"Nobody had to know. It didn't need to be that piece. There's plenty of other stuff up there. Anything could have been dropped. It just happened that the murderer found that piece nearest the edge and used it. He could have used something that had been up there for ages."

"All the same, you're pointing all possible suspicion in your own direction. You won't talk about anyone but 'they.' Are you so scared of 'they' that you'll even take the fall for them before you'll talk?"

"I am scared," Bartholomew said. "Who wouldn't be? They got Peters. They got that bartender fellow. They can be thinking that they have to get me. They're certainly watching me unless it was you who had that thing dumped against my door. It could have been you."

"Why would I do that?"

"You think I know more than I'm telling you. You can be trying to make me think my safety will lie in talking to you. So you might do it just to make me feel threatened when I'm not."

"Don't kid yourself, Bartholomew. You are threatened."

The inspector was back at feeding the man the pitch he had been throwing at him all the way downtown in the car. He was in danger and his only way out of it would be through cooperating with the inspector on catching the killer and putting him away where he could do no harm.

In the car such arguments had drawn nothing but obstinate silence. Now they brought on the all-too-con-

venient response. Killers go out on bail and even before they have come to trial they kill again. Killers con-
victed and jailed are released on parole to kill again.
Killers have gangster friends and associates and even
while in jail they can enlist such people to kill for
them. So where is the safety in cooperating with the
police?

Schmitty countered with his conventional argument.
As long as anything that can be told remains untold,
there can be gain in silencing a man who has not yet
spoken. Once he has spoken, the profit has gone out of
silencing him. It's a good argument, but to it there is
also the conventional response. A man can be killed in
revenge. A man can be killed as a punishment for talking and as a warning to others against talking.

"Why was the bartender killed? Why was he delivered to my door?"

"He was killed," Schmitty said, "because there was
something he should have told me and didn't. He was
killed before he could change his mind, before he
might decide to talk. He was delivered as a warning to
you to keep silent. So you keep silent as he did and
then the time comes when your 'they' for one reason or
another come to think you may be wavering. They'll
knock you off before you can get to me."

"You're the one who has done this to me," Bartholomew wailed. "If you had only left me alone."

Schmitty shrugged. "Okay," he said. "You leave me
only one thing to do. I am putting you under arrest for
the murder of Paul Peters. If you did it, then it will be
a good arrest. If you didn't, then at least I can give you
protection until your attorney here gets you out and
brings you back into danger."

Bartholomew protested that the inspector couldn't

do it. The attorney backed his client up. Schmitty, nevertheless, did do it, and when the attorney hurried off to set in motion the machinery to bring about his client's release, Schmitty left Bartholomew to sweat.

We headed back uptown. I was giving it as my opinion that Bartholomew had still not come completely clean. Schmitty agreed but in his estimation Bartholomew had told all he was going to tell.

"I'll need some new facts to throw at him," he said, "before there's a hope that he'll break down and come through with the rest of it."

"A confession?"

"Or an identification. That 'they' of his isn't nearly enough."

"Where are we going now?"

"To talk to the one man I still need to hear from. The boys have located Hank Lusk. We're paying him a visit."

"Lusk? P.P.'s Henry. Is he the other man? Is he the one who helped Bartholomew with the delivery?"

"Or he knows who did."

"It could have been Rich Dawson. It could have been Jocko."

"They had other jobs. Hank was P.P.'s man of all work."

"But it could have been anyone."

"Probably enlisted by Lusk or engaged by him."

"And he picked a wrong one?"

"Lusks don't know anybody but wrong ones."

"And you expect him to tell you when Bartholomew won't?" I asked.

"Bartholomew's scared. Do you think Hank can be scared? He was closest to the dead man. There's only one thing that can keep him from talking."

"Wanting to handle it himself," I said. "Vengeance is mine and all that."

"Nowhere near as good a silencer as fear," the inspector said.

We drove up to an apartment house on Amsterdam Avenue. That's a neighborhood in transition. There was a time when it was upper-middle and the apartments were well built—solid and spacious. The neighborhood slid into a long decline and where there had been a considerable degree of luxury there came decay into a slum. It was never a reasonable development. It was good housing and in one of Manhattan's convenient locations.

In recent years, as the pressure for good Manhattan housing has increased greatly, the process has been going into reverse. They call it gentrification, but it's a new generation of upper-middles moving in. They repair and renovate to bring the neighborhood back to something like it once was. It is only something like because these new people have a tolerance and a free-and-easy spirit unknown to the solid and stolid bourgeoisie of the earlier day.

Curiously, however, even in that earlier day it had been a neighborhood favored by prosperous gangsters. A few killings amid the plush and glitter of some of those apartment house lobbies may have been one of the elements that started the neighborhood into its slide.

I had the thought that it might have been a little old-fashioned on the part of P.P.'s Henry to be living in that area. Affluent gangsters had for some time been turning up in the part of town across the park known as "the fashionable upper East Side," but it occurred to me that Lusk might well be not quite that affluent.

The building at which the inspector pulled up indicated as much. Even though it was one of the good, solid, old jobs, it had gone only partway on its climb back up to elegance. There was no doorman. The lobby door was not locked. There was no attendant in the lobby. The lobby, nevertheless, wasn't empty. Two men were there and I recognized both of them. They were a pair of the inspector's Homicide boys.

"He's up there?" Schmitty asked.

"11C. Around here he calls himself Herbert Leary."

The boys joined us in the elevator and rode up to the eleventh floor with us.

"Alias," I said, "but he keeps the initials."

"They mostly do," one of the lads said. "It makes it easier for them to remember."

"That's part of it," the inspector said. "But the ones like Hank are monogram crazy—monogrammed cuff links, monogrammed shirts. Didn't you notice? You didn't get to see the monograms on the underwear, but he has them and aliases can't stray off the monograms."

Up on the eleventh floor it was evident that, quite apart from not straying off his monograms, Lusk hadn't been going to stray in any other respect. He hadn't been easy to locate, but once he'd been found, the inspector had arranged to keep him pinned down. A couple more of the Homicide people popped out of the service-stairs area. The inspector waved them back. While we came to the front door of 11C, Lusk was not going to have any open road out of the apartment's service door. Schmitty rang.

The door remained shut, but Lusk shouted through it.

"What do you want?"

"Talk."

"Cops. I don't talk to cops."

"Open up."

"What for?"

"To save us breaking the door down."

"I don't save you shit."

Dropping out of this shouted exchange, the inspector lowered his voice. "He thinks Bartholomew talked," he said. "He's wrong about that, but it makes no difference because he's right about what we've come for. It's an easy door, but I want this careful. He has a gun and he'll use it. He's not going to just wait in there and let us break in to take him on the murder charge."

"Henry?" I said. "He was P.P.'s man."

"He's a gun for hire," the inspector said. "When a man hires muscle, he has to be smart and watch it. He can't expect loyalty. His man can always be hired out from under him by a higher bidder. His man can also get ambitious on his own."

"But there's Drew," I said. "There's Dawson. There's Bartholomew. There are all those big, husky girls."

"On your testimony, kid, it has to be Hank," Schmitty said. Then, raising his voice again, he shouted through the door. "Open up or we're coming through."

"And you'll get your damn heads blown off."

The inspector turned back to me. "On what I've had from you," he said, "I've known it was Lusk. To prove it on him I needed more. Once he starts shooting, that will be it. Just the fact that he's doing it will give me all I need."

"If he doesn't blow your head off," I said.

"That'll be the day."

He was examining the lock on the apartment door. Nodding with satisfaction, he brought out a bunch of keys and selected the one he wanted. It was a master that would work the lock. He fitted it into the keyhole. Everyone was standing back. Flattened against the wall beside the door, he had only his hand in what could have been the line of fire.

I realized that it was most unlikely that, shooting through the door, Lusk would hit the inspector's hand. To aim in that area would mean that he would be shooting his own lock out. I couldn't conceive of his doing that.

As soon as the inspector started turning the key, the shots came. Lusk had been listening. He'd heard the grating of the key in the lock. Slugs came through the door, but there was nobody in their path. The inspector and his men returned the fire. To me it seemed a futile gesture since it was a virtual certainty that Lusk would have jumped out of range, but I was wrong. The slugs going through the door from both sides opened holes.

A tear-gas canister was brought up and the gas was fed in through one of the bullet holes. There were a few shots while the gas was going in but then they stopped and there was nothing to hear but the sounds of coughing and strangling. It was only a matter of moments before the door burst open and someone came out into Schmitty's arms. It wasn't Lusk. It was one of The Topless Towers. Out of costume without being into much of anything else, she was all but naked. I recognized her. She was the one to whom I had not delivered P.P.'s message. It was Cynthia.

Schmitty handed her over to one of his men and waited. Nothing happened.

"Drop your gun and come out."

He had to repeat the order a couple of times. With

the door now open, he was able to add to that order the enforcement of a couple of gas grenades lobbed into the apartment. The increased gas concentration did it. Hank Lusk came out and he came unarmed.

Some of the puzzle by then had come clear for me. I could now see a motive. Along with Peters, Lusk had lusted after Cynthia. She was his and Peters would have been taking her away from him. Lusk had taken the one way open to him for stopping that. That much I had, but it seemed thin. Also I still couldn't imagine in what way I had tipped the inspector to him.

Lusk had, of course, acted for Peters in the purchase and delivery of the St. George group. He had enlisted Jocko to the extent of inducing the bartender to feed me the mickey. If I wasn't police, I was close to it. The Face had made that much clear. I had to be out of the way. Lusk hadn't expected that the mickey would take such quick effect. It had backfired on him, leaving me much in the way. Jocko had brought me in from the street. Lusk had kicked me to make sure I was thoroughly out and, satisfied of that, he had dragged me out to the alley.

With that he had taken care of everything, but for his safety he was left dependent on the silence of two people. Jocko, he'd expected, would not talk. The hired accomplice doesn't jeopardize his own skin. That left Bartholomew, and he could tell that Lusk had handled the purchase and assisted in the delivery of the St. George and the dragon. It had been Lusk's judgment that Bartholomew could be terrified into peddling any story Lusk would feed him and that fear of Lusk would keep him in line. In that, of course, Hank had been right. Andy B. had been sticking to his story.

As the thing developed, however, Jocko had been

the weaker link. Ethel had seen Jocko carry me into the club. What she had seen placed Jocko on the scene after the killing had been done, and Ethel was talking to the police. In that situation skin-saving had taken on a new dimension. Jocko couldn't be expected to take the fall alone, so Jocko had to go.

I had that much of it sorted out, but what had I told Inspector Schmidt that convinced him Lusk was his man? I never could figure that out. I had to wait till the first quiet moment and then I asked Schmitty to explain.

"It's simple," he said. "Peters was out in the alley waiting for the girls. Lusk wasn't out there with him. You saw him inside the club while you were lapping up your mickey. What could he have been doing in the club?"

"Getting me set up?"

"No. Jocko was taking care of that for him. Peters was at the back door. Lusk was watching the front. He saw what he was supposed to be watching for. All exits were being made through the front. Why then would Lusk leave Peters in the alley to wait for the girls who wouldn't be coming through there? Why didn't he stop Cynthia and hold her for Peters?"

"Rich Dawson would have taken him apart," I said.

"Against Hank's gun? Lusk had the gun. He'd pulled it on you, or can you have forgotten that?"

"I haven't forgotten."

"Also, even if you could be right about Dawson's effectiveness, Dawson wouldn't have stopped his telling Peters that his bird had flown. Hank didn't tell Peters. He left him waiting in the alley, left him there till he could drop the dragon's tail on him."

Once the inspector has his man and he can concentrate his digging, other items emerge. I had felt that the motive was thin and it was. Since, however, it was only part of the motive, it was enough. It developed that Lusk had been playing financial games, stealing from Peters regularly. That operation had reached dimensions that had even The Golden Creep asking questions.

When you ask a Hank Lusk such questions, you had better be in a strong defensive position.

ABOUT THE AUTHOR

George Bagby is the pen name of an author who has been honored with the Grand Master Award, the Mystery Writers of America's highest distinction. He has been writing crime novels since 1935. He was born in Manhattan and has always lived there, when not on world travels. The most recent adventures of Bagby and Inspector Schmidt of the New York Police Department are *The Sitting Duck, A Question of Quarry, Country and Fatal,* and *Mugger's Day.*